I0723044

delights *and* disappointments

Larry Boyd

Acknowledgements

I wish to acknowledge the invaluable work of my editor, Pamela Oddy, without whose suggestions, insights and patience this collection of stories would be the lesser. Also, I am indebted to the members of Fusion Theatre in Dandenong with whom I worked as director in building performances which appear here in the story Contes de Fées. I also acknowledge the four members of Wheel Women with whom I worked for three years developing the play Perfectly Imperfect. They were Janette Lee, Mel Smith, Deborah Humphries and Marie Ireland. Finally, I would not be able to write without the continued support of my much-published partner, Barbara Caine, with whom I have many amazing conversations about writing, the world of politics and the performing arts.

This book is dedicated to Pamela Oddy

Delights and Disappointments
Print ISBN: 9781761099113
Ebook ISBN: 9781761097027
Copyright © text Larry Boyd 2025
Cover design by Graham Davidson

First published 2025 by
Ginninderra Press
PO Box 2 Bentleigh 3204
ginninderrapress.com.au

Contents

The Golden Web

Beatrice's magnificent golden web shimmered in the bright sunlight. She looked over the intricately connected threads with satisfaction at the perfect geometry of the design. Ah, she sighed. I spin gold threads to weave my home like all Nephila. My golden web is strong and beautiful. It is my orb.

These were private thoughts. She never spoke them aloud, always cognisant of the irony in Minerva's punishment of Arachne, a punishment which, by bringing the arachnids into existence, was seen by the golden orb as her good fortune.

The contented spider sat in the middle of her orb, still as any golden silk weaver can ever be. Her web hung high between two flowering crepe myrtles, high enough to capture insects flying by. Two smaller spiders had set themselves up on this same glittering structure. Beatrice didn't mind. Golden orb weaving spiders are docile creatures and so long as her larder hanging above her head was full and safe, she didn't mind the intruders.

Her carapace was full with her babies waiting to be born and she had been assiduous in capturing enough food for herself and her mate and to nourish the little spiderlings when they came. The cocoon above her head was full of flies, beetles and even a European honey bee. There were also three mosquitoes which would be a lovely appetiser before she and her mate devoured the honey bee.

Beatrice loved her life. It was a fairy tale existence in a private garden, an almost magical place with wide, green lawns and lush with frangipanis, hibiscus, ginger and other flowering plants that drew in the pollinators. It was those little flying creatures that were the spice of life for a spider.

Enchanted by fairy tales, Beatrice looked forward to warm days when the children would come into the garden with their mother or a grandparent who would read to them. The family would gather in the shade of the crepe myrtles. There would be snacks and drinks, but nothing as delicious as a big blowfly or a wasp.

The stories in Ovid's *Metamorphoses* were a great favorite, especially that of Minerva punishing Arachne for her proud boasting that her weavings were better than those of the goddess. The little ones would oooh and aaah at the big spider's web strung across the trees above their heads. They could look, but were forbidden to touch.

The stories always made Beatrice feel that her life was the best ever fairy tale, secure as she was in her golden world. What delighted her most was that she saw herself as being part of a world of women who spun. Queens, princesses, maids, stepmothers and witches all spin in fairy tales. There is a lot of unhappiness in those tales, she conceded. Pricked fingers, punishments at the wheel, weird little imps extracting a promise from a girl to spin gold in return for her first born. But the stories always had happy endings.

What didn't enchant her were the noisy rows that frequently took place in the lane running along the back of the garden. Sometimes there would be shouting and a human would be pushed roughly against the fence, shaking it and alarming Beatrice and the other spiders. But the shouting always died down and the troublemakers moved off.

One day when Beatrice was close to her time to give birth, there was a terrible ruckus in the laneway. She could hear angry shouting and someone being pushed and punched. The birds and spiders in the garden took fright and fled to hide in trees. Before she could traverse her own web in escape, Beatrice saw a dark shadow vaulting over the fence. The body hurtled onto her web, tearing it down, dislodging her. As a boot came down on her, crushing her underfoot, she had the fleeting thought that not all fairy tales have a happy ending.

Contes des Fées

'No,' Abby repeated for the umpteenth time that year. She glanced around the black walls of the theatre where she was wanting to create Bluebeard's castle for the year's production. 'We are not going to have anyone wearing a blue beard in our play. Danny is playing the main character and he doesn't have a blue beard, does he?'

'W…w…we…we…we could ma…ma…mak… We could make one,' Verity rushed out in one breath. The whole group went into holding mode whenever Verity spoke because her stutter was so bad.

'We could make one,' Tilly repeated with a sense of wonderment, even though the suggestion seemed to have come up at every workshop.

'We don't need to,' Abby said, doubling down on her rising sense of frustration.

She hadn't much experience in doing drama with people with special needs and she had never done a whole production. Initially, she had said no to her friend Georgie, Bright Sparks Theatre Ensemble's artistic director, who had planned a year off to travel and check out drama projects for disabled people in other countries. Then she'd thought about it again. I don't have much coming up this year. This would be a nice little filler to tide me over for a few months. I guess I can manage one production. It's only for a year. It'll be good experience. So she had agreed, so long as Georgie was prepared to kick off the workshop and provide ongoing support from the sidelines until she left.

Only then did Georgie drop the Bluebeard bombshell.

'Bluebeard?! That's a bit heavy, isn't it?'

But no matter how hard Abby argued against it, Georgie always came back with 'The group decided on this last year. I read them the story. They're up for it.' She grinned at Abby. 'It's a fairy tale actually.

The original tales were pretty grim until Disney got onto them and prettied them up.

'Over the year, you and the group collaborate to devise the play in a series of workshops. Take masses of notes. I use my laptop. Then,' she went on to explain, 'when you've got a clear narrative, you write the script from what's been agreed and that's what you rehearse.'

The first workshops of the year had been a testing ground for Abby but she felt she had learned a lot with Georgie's support. She was used to being very directive in productions she had done in the past. However, with Bright Sparks Theatre Ensemble the process was different.

'You have to be inclusive in your approach,' Georgie had said.

'What does that mean – "inclusive"?' Abby had asked. 'Am I supposed to give all of them leading roles?'

Georgie roared with laughter. 'God, no. You work to their ability. Each of the members has something to contribute so you find a way of working that into the script, then into the show.'

Abby shook her head. 'What if they can't do what I'm asking for? Like, I couldn't have Sleeper, the Prader-Willi guy, playing a handsome prince charming.'

'Why not?'

Abby laughed, then coloured as she realised Georgie wasn't joking.

Georgie was thoughtful, weighing up her words. 'It's important to be non-judgemental, Abby. Validate them. Always be friendly, make them feel good about what they are doing, about themselves. It's their project, not ours. Of course you have to set standards, but don't expect the guys always to meet them. Princesses can be in wheelchairs with cerebral palsy, super-heroes can be struggling with Prader-Willi or severe cognitive impairment. Think about drama differently. The magic of theatre transforms these people when they act. The whole aim of this project is to be transformative.'

Acting on this advice made progress much slower than Abby was used to, but after a number of workshops and debriefing sessions with Georgie, she found her reservoir of patience and began to go with the flow. Though, she privately admitted to herself, Verity's stuttering tested her to the limits.

Then Georgie had flown out of Australia and Abby was on her own.

'Ma…ma…ma…'

Verity was trying to make a point again, but all Abby wanted to do was get on with the workshop. As Verity turned to her, a wicked grin spread across her face. She put her hands under her chin and wriggled her fingers. It was an approximation of a beard and it was rather funny. Sleeper rolled his eyes and shook his head at Abby.

'We decided against that, Verity,' Abby smiled, 'don't you remember? We discussed it at the beginning of the year.'

Danny suddenly stood up and played a furious riff on an imaginary guitar.

'Danny!' Tilly exclaimed, placing a restraining hand on his arm. 'Sit down.'

Danny ignored her and continued the guitar solo as the rest of the group looked on unperturbed. God help us, Abby thought. She'd cast Danny in the lead role.

Bright Sparks had done a number of plays over the few years since it had been founded. Their performance abilities and understanding of stagecraft had developed extraordinarily under Georgie's guidance and training. It was the level of unpredictability that got at Abby. She never knew what to expect next from the group, but knew as sure as hell that some new interruption would come.

'Okay,' she said. 'Let's say it one more time. Danny will not wear a beard, not blue or yellow or purple, not anything. What the people in our story are frightened of is his disability and the fact that his wives keep disappearing. That's scary, yeah?'

Abby had no idea whether they had understood the concept behind the production or not. How do I get them to make the connection? she wondered. To understand that our play is about disability, not someone with a blue beard?

The issue of discrimination against people with disability had come up at the first workshop of the year. Amy started it by recounting being abused at the shops by a group of girls who mocked her Down's syndrome appearance, her weight and walk. 'Spazzo!' they sneered at her, 'Retard!' 'You waddle like a duck.' They had laughed, mimicked Amy's gait and moved on, leaving her on the verge of tears.

'What people don't like about our Bluebeard is his disability,' Abby persisted. 'You know, all those things you talked about in February, the way some people can be mean to you.'

'February?' someone called out, incredulous. It was as if the month was another alien idea.

Abby was rifling through her notes, looking for their earlier comments about episodes of rudeness they had experienced. I need to find a different approach to help them understand the switch from a blue beard to disability. Georgie had told her that the idea of the beard had tickled their fancy when she read the Perrault version of the Bluebeard story to them, but some of the group hadn't let go of the beard idea.

Danny shot up out of his chair. Danny was autistic, a short man, slim and with a pointed face. He adopted his usual stance with his head turned away from the group at about thirty degrees, facing the ceiling with a look of sublime clarity transforming his otherwise fierce features. 'I get it. I won't have a blue beard. I'll just be me.' He cocked his head a little as if he was waiting for a response from the ceiling.

Abby felt a surge of relief. 'Brilliant, Danny, you get it,' she smiled, nodding and looking around the group to gauge their response to Danny's moment of enlightenment.

Abby's heart sank. Cheryl was at the back fiddling with her hair, trying to put it into a ponytail with a scrunchy. Sleeper was rummaging in his bag looking for a snack as usual. He had Prader-Willi and therefore shouldn't be eating between meals. Abby was caught between checking Sleeper's impulse to eat and not wanting to lose the momentum of Danny's enlightenment moment. Andy was rocking from foot to foot mouthing the words 'get it, get it' while Sandy was looking at Danny with something just short of adoration.

Danny was a perfect choice for the main role. His form of autism gave a sharpness to his characterisation of the murderous duke. Danny almost didn't have to act. As he had said, I'll just be me. He was edgy, unpredictable, at times scary when he let fly with his razor-sharp voice. What was even weirder was when he stood quietly, head crooked, staring past you as he listened to what you were saying with a palpable intensity. He wasn't aggressive to the others. In fact, sometimes Abby wondered how aware of the others Danny was. His introversion kept him locked in a world of private conversations and sudden pronouncements to somebody who existed for him alone. He would occasionally burst into song or act out his pantomime of being a rock musician.

Along with his eccentricities, Danny was clever. He had learnt the dialogue the group had devised and which Abby had drafted and fine-tuned. He knew the blocking and never made a false move on stage. And he had not baulked at doing a choreographed dance with one of the other guys who played the servant. That had been one of Georgie's proposals.

The other unresolved issue in the group was Scotty. Scotty was the mystery member. He attended every workshop without fail, but never joined in the drama activities. At the beginning of the year, Abby had found Scotty sitting on the floor, propping up a wall, with his hoodie pulled so far down on his head that Abby had no idea what he looked like.

'Yeah, that's Scott,' Julie, the carer who brought the group to the theatre, had commented nonchalantly when Abby asked about him. 'He's always like that,' she'd advised, 'totally withdrawn. He won't come good. Don't factor him into a role.'

So what about the inclusiveness Georgie had talked about? Abby asked herself. It was the kind of I-don't-give-a-damn response that bugged her. Then why bring him? she wanted to say. This is a serious training program, not babysitting. Serious training program! Who am

I kidding? It's a community activity. Disability arts. Disability drama. About as unsexy as you can get. I don't like him sitting there doing nothing, but he's not my responsibility and apparently he isn't hers. Poor bugger, nobody's man.

It was during the third term that the group finally seemed to get what the play was more or less about. Choreographing the ball scene had been a clincher. The guys loved dancing and they all had a role to play in the big wedding party scene. The rehearsals were going well, but Abby was constantly nagged by the question of how Bluebeard managed to get away with killing all those wives, dragging them into the room at the end of the hall and hanging them up on the wall. He must have had help, like a devoted servant or someone, she calculated. That's a perfect scenario for a dance sequence, a pas de deux for the two guys. But I've already cast all the group into roles. There isn't anybody left to do that part.

That's the trouble with fairy tales, Abby reflected. The storytellers never bother to fill in the details. Like, how did Cinderella get home when the carriage turned back into a pumpkin? And she had no shoes? How did the ugly sisters get stitched up after one had a toe and the other her heel cut off? How come they didn't die of septicaemia or gangrene? And the really big question, who tended to Snow White's bodily functions while she was asleep all that time? She giggled, unaware that the ensemble was watching her.

'Hey, Miss Director.' Danny's voice snapped Abby out of her reverie.

'Sorry, Danny. Sorry, everyone.'

Julie came and stood next to her, a questioning look on her face. 'Problem?'

'No, yeah.' What she really wanted was time out to think about the servant problem. However, that wasn't possible in the middle of a workshop. If they took a break now, the momentum would be lost. There was still time to work on other parts of the play that needed consolidation.

'Sorry,' she muttered again, 'but what I'm thinking is that Bluebeard must have had help to hide what he had done to those women, a servant, something like that.'

'Ah!' Julie nodded. 'And who's going to do that?' she asked.

'That's the question. I'll have to ask one of the cast to do a double role,' Abby murmured. 'I know they hate that kind of thing. As it is, it takes so much concentration on their part to learn dialogue and the moves let alone cope with a major addition like this.'

Julie looked dubious. She opened her mouth to say something, but Abby wasn't in the mood for a discussion with her. 'There has to be a servant,' she said and turned back to the group.

'I've just had a thought.' Abby hesitated, knowing that she was probably about to torpedo the group's concentration for the rest of the workshop. 'Don't you think Bluebeard must have had a servant to help him with the dead wives?'

Some members were staring with their mouths open, others looked blank, while Danny turned his head towards the ceiling and whispered to himself, 'Servant?'

'Wha…wha… Wha…what is a…is a…a servant? Verity sat up straight, but her eyes were somehow out of focus.

Abby wasn't sure if she was looking at her or sinking back into her own little world. You know what a servant is. You're playing games here. This isn't the time, Verity, she thought with more than a touch of impatience.

It was unmistakable, but none of the cast seemed to hear Danny hiss through his teeth, 'Stupid!'

Move on, Abby told herself as Verity's eyes refocused and she turned her glare on Danny.

'A servant is a sort of helper, Verity,' she said quickly, short-circuiting any possible altercation between the two, 'and I really need someone to play Bluebeard's servant – you know, someone who helped him with the murders.'

She paused, then asked as brightly as she could, 'Who's willing to do two roles?'

Cheryl had taken off her scrunchy and was attempting to put her hair back in a ponytail. 'Murders?' she gasped, the scrunchy suspended in mid-air. 'What murders?'

Abby felt an urge to end the workshop there and then. She took a deep breath, sensing Julie preparing to interrupt with one of her unhelpful pieces of advice.

She stepped into the middle of the group. 'Anyone up for a second role?'

There was a resounding silence from the group. As she moved around, raising an eyebrow at possible candidates, each avoided looking at her.

'No, not me.'

'No way, José.'

Katie buried her head in Sue's lap and Wally suddenly had to go to the toilet.

'Come on, guys. We need someone,' Abby pleaded. 'Sleeper, you could do that. It's a good role for you.'

Sleeper smirked. 'You are kidding, aren't you?'

Danny's girlfriend Tilly piped up, 'You do it, Abby!'

There was a cheer of support from some of the group. Then someone called out 'No!' and that was supported by murmurs of disapproval from a couple of others.

'Yes,' Tilly insisted.

'Sit down, Tilly,' Danny roared, but she ignored him.

'Abby, you do it.' Tilly stood looking at her, waiting.

'I'm the director, Tilly. I don't do the acting.'

'Sorry,' Tilly shrugged.

'Sit down, Tilly.' Danny roared so commandingly and loudly you would be forgiven for thinking that Tilly was on the other side of town.

'It's okay, Danny. Tilly has tried to help us. Thanks, Tilly.' Abby smiled at her. I'm not up for this today, she thought. She flashed a broad smile at the group. 'Now, who else…'

Sleeper called out from the back of the group. 'I'll do it.'

The group turned round, staring at Sleeper. Sandy turned back to face the front. Her eyes were wide and staring at the floor, disbelief frozen across her face. The group slowly turned back to face Abby, watching for her reaction to Sleeper's change of heart.

'N…n…n…no wa…no wa…'

Verity, you could turn a person psychopathic, Abby thought. She managed a smile at Verity, but held up her hand, cutting the girl off.

Georgie had warned her that in past productions, Sleeper was never on the same page as others in the group. He would amble slowly around the stage, hauling his body to a place where he usually ended up out of position and would deliver lines that he should have spoken in a previous scene or a scene yet to happen. Yet he was smart. He knew his lines, knew the names of everybody in the company.

Abby fluctuated between thinking that Sleeper simply didn't get drama and the suspicion that for some reason he deliberately did the wrong thing out of spite. The latter thought was reinforced when some of Sleeper's mates occasionally wandered in towards the end of a workshop and stood smugly watching and muttering slyly under their breath. Abby never heard what they said, but suspected they were inwardly laughing at the members of the group. But now she was on a spot and had to accept Sleeper's offer. After all, she had asked Sleeper directly.

The notion of choreographing a dance between Danny and Sleeper seemed to Abby to be beyond her. Whereas Danny was lithe, agile and energetic, Sleeper was sluggish and inflexible, carrying so much weight that it immobilised him. It wasn't Sleeper's fault, simply a fact of the Prader-Willi condition.

I have to accept all of that, Abby told herself. This is an inclusive program. Sleeper has volunteered so I have to put him in the role of the faithful servant. But she couldn't help cursing herself for bringing up the issue of a servant at all.

Then, as sometimes happens in the stress of a moment, Abby had what she considered a brainwave. Sleeper can simply stand there gesturing with his hands where Danny has to dance to and I'll choreograph the steps for Danny alone. Disappointing, for sure; it would have been more fun to have the two men dance together, but this idea should work. Sleeper will be like a puppet-master directing Danny's movements. Not quite the power balance you'd expect in Bluebeard's house, but hey, any port in a storm.

Abby stood up and clapped her hands. 'Thank you, Sleeper. We have a manservant, ladies and gentlemen. Now let's get back to work. We'll start by practising the dance for the ball then begin blocking the scene where Bluebeard looks at his dead wives.'

The weeks passed. Winter turned into spring and the show was looking good. Danny and Elyssa were great as Bluebeard and the new wife. The ball scene was more or less working, though Tim usually wandered off, breaking the line and leaving his partner frustrated. Even Sleeper had more or less adapted to the dance sequence.

Then the unthinkable happened. Sleeper told Abby, 'I don't want to do drama any more.' He picked up his bag and walked out.

Abby was gutted to see Sleeper's mates sniggering outside the theatre.

Everyone was shocked. Danny launched into a tirade against Sleeper which Abby had to spend some time short-circuiting while Cheryl comforted Tilly, who had burst into tears.

'Should we cancel the performance?' Julie asked.

Those who heard her cried out, 'No!'

'No way.' Abby couldn't have been more adamant. 'Not after all the hard work these guys have put in.'

The cast was looking at her, waiting for her to sort it out. But she couldn't. Having cast a role for Sleeper, it was almost impossible to unpick the onstage interactions with his character in a way which would keep the momentum of the show flowing smoothly. Keeping the flow going was always an issue, even at the best of times. She thought of the massive effort everyone had made. I've got to make this work, somehow.

Gloom had settled on the cast. It was as dark and heavy as the black curtains draped along the walls.

This is not good, Abby told herself. 'Come on, guys, let's run the dance scene between Bluebeard and the servant. I'll fill in for the servant for the moment. Let's go, Danny.' She turned to Julie. 'Can you get the Ross Edwards track on the CD player ready to go? I think it's track seven.'

Everyone moved into position. There were grumblings against Sleeper. There was a lack of energy, a sense of defeat that held them all in its thrall. Abby turned to the carer and nodded. The music started, but Danny stood motionless. Abby moved to him and took his arm the way Sleeper had learned to do.

Danny stared at Abby, that sideways look which didn't seem to take the person in at all. Then someone was beside them. Abby and Danny turned as one.

Scotty was standing there. His hoodie was off his head and Abby saw his face for the first time. Scotty was beautiful. His delicate features, his dark eyelashes, the thick head of dark hair, the lips and the slight flush of pink on his pale cheeks were the miracle Abby hadn't thought could happen. Scotty stared at her, not saying anything, but looking as if he would bolt in seconds if something didn't happen.

Abby stepped aside, leaving Danny and Scotty together, centre stage. God, he doesn't even know the role, Abby fretted. Let's just get through this afternoon then I can rethink this over the next week.

'Really? You?' Danny was giving Scotty one of his sidelong looks. 'Just follow me, man.'

Abby turned to Julie. 'From the beginning of the track,' she called.

The track began again.

Everyone watched spellbound as Danny and Scotty performed the dance. Scotty pulled the upstage curtain aside to reveal the stuffed dummies hanging on the back wall. He gently eased Bluebeard back to the upright after each contraction of anguish at seeing the bodies of the murdered wives. At the end of the scene, he pulled the curtain closed and danced Bluebeard back into the hall of the castle.

Unbelievable, Abby thought. All that time sitting on the ground, hiding under your hoodie, and yet you've been watching, absorbing and learning the play and its moves. And now you're improvising in the dance, filling the gaps that Sleeper could never do. Unbelievable!

The cast had come over to the two men, congratulating them and patting their backs. Danny extricated himself, avoiding physical contact. Scotty blushed scarlet and kept bobbing above the heads to look at Abby. Presumably he was looking for some sign of approval. Abby grinned and gave Scotty two thumbs up. God, she thought, have we got a show or what?

Weeks later, the first night performance was good. Not perfect, but very good. Most of the mistakes went unnoticed by the audience, who gave the group a standing ovation. As they took their bows, Abby grinned to see Verity standing in line, waggling her fingers under her chin.

Danny was sensational, but Abby felt the quiet achiever of the night was Scotty. The young man blushed the entire performance, but he didn't make one slip-up.

There was one more feel-good moment that night after the final act. The cast was in the dressing rooms changing out of their costumes, washing their faces and packing their bags. Julie had called Abby to the foyer where the directors of the day centre wanted to congratulate her. They were talking when a stranger came up and spoke.

'I'm Danny's father.'

'Hey, pleased to meet you,' Abby grinned and they shook hands.

'Just tell me how you did it?' Danny's father asked.

Abby looked puzzled.

'I can't get him to do a thing at home and you've got him speaking lines, dancing, doing the sword fight at the end of the play without maiming anyone. How?'

When the laughter subsided Abby ventured, 'The magic of theatre?'

Abby was the last to leave. She had gone around the dressing rooms, gathering up props, bits of costume, bags and an assortment of brushes, combs, hairpins and ribbons. She turned out the lights in the dressing rooms and walked into the auditorium.

She looked at the stage, recalling the performance and the many memorable moments in it, good and bad. A smile settled on her face. Images of the cast members as they bid her goodnight rose in her mind. Everywhere there was joy, happiness, the sense of satisfaction on their faces and this was reflected on the faces of parents, family, carers and friends.

A few weeks before the show opened she had joined some girl-friends in a local pub. She was tired, dispirited and concerned at how the rehearsals had taken a turn for the worse. That happens in all theatre, she told them. The cast goes flat after a long rehearsal period. This has been almost a year. No wonder they're over it.

'Why are you doing it?' Biddy asked.

'Is it worth it?' Roberta had added.

As Abby turned off the lights in the auditorium and closed its doors, those words came back to her. 'Is it worth it?'

'You betcha! I love it,' she sang to the empty foyer and danced across to the outer doors, set the locks and stepped out into the moonlight.

The Tutor Tutored

'Have you read the book?' Doug sat at the large wooden table, waiting expectantly for the girl sitting opposite to answer.

It was his first time at the house where a small number of kids at risk lived under the care of a charitable organisation. The director of the facility had contacted him through a mutual friend, an older and experienced teacher who had mentored Doug in his first year out in the classroom. The thought of making a difference excited him, so he had readily accepted the offer to tutor at the house.

The girl opposite had draped herself languorously across the table after sinking onto a chair. As he stared at her, she shifted into what approximated to an upright sitting posture. Doug smiled inwardly at the performative nature of the movement and followed her gaze as she looked around the room.

'This room,' he had been told by house parent Zoe on a tour of inspection when he first arrived, 'is the study.'

Hmm, he thought. Study eh? No books, no pictures on the wall, maps, in fact, nothing to stimulate the imagination. So what is she looking at? He turned his attention back to the girl.

Some of the dingy classrooms at his school, overcrowded with noisy teenagers, came to his mind. At least this room is light and spacious. That's got to be a plus. He raised a questioning eyebrow at the girl, but she didn't say anything. Avoiding looking at him, her eyes drifted past him to the passage outside.

He followed her gaze to the double doors opening onto the side passage where earlier he had noticed a random assortment of plants thriving in terracotta pots. The plants were a greening concession to the cream walls of the house and the grey path. Well, someone's got a green thumb he decided, but I don't think it's this girl. Is she high on something?

He glanced at the terracotta pots to see if there was marijuana growing. Spying a mix of basil, thyme and coriander in one of them, he drew in a deep breath, trying to catch a whiff of herbal aroma. Maybe she had a joint before the lesson? I should have asked Zoe.

Zoe had slipped out of the study after introducing Sharna to Doug. A phone had started ringing in the house and it rang and rang. If there were any other kids around, they weren't answering it despite Zoe shouting up the passage for someone to pick up.

Doug returned his attention to Sharna. 'Have you? Read the novel, I mean?'

'Nah!'

'You haven't read it, okay.' Doug looked at the girl as she slowly turned her head, focusing her large hazel eyes on him.

Hazel and speckled with green and gold lights, her irises were like little treasure troves of rare jewels. She lowered her eyelids, a slow covering of the treasures, concealing them from view. The brown eyelashes were like fairy locks, fine, glossy, strong, sealing the lids, daring him to kiss them. Then she opened her eyes. The fairy locks were released, the lids lifted upwards and there they were: the jewels.

Jewels, fairy locks! This is crazy stuff. Why did I think of kissing her eyes open? Doug was struggling to get a sense of her. She's being deliberately provocative, he decided. Is she checking me out?

On an intake of breath, a contraction of his loins, Doug became acutely aware that he was reacting physically to her allure. He felt his heart skip a beat. He inhaled deeply and blew out the breath with a sustained deliberation, a face-saver, a distraction. A look came into Sharna's eyes. What is that? he asked himself.

The afternoon light glowed through the window behind Sharna, turning her incandescent with its brightness. He shifted his chair away, protecting his eyes from the direct sunlight and Sharna's tantalising gaze. What is that look?

She's taking in everything about me, appraising me. He felt a deep flush enflaming his skin, felt its heat spread down his neck and tickle his chest. She's bloody hot, she knows it and she's sizing me up. He looked away quickly and placed his fingers on the book.

Her gaze dropped to the book. Or was she looking at his fingers? He quickly took his hand away and dropped it onto his lap. No, he thought, don't do that, and quickly put both hands back on the book.

'So you haven't read it. Okay. Do you think you might? Read the book, I mean?'

She folded her arms on the table and rested her head on them, looking up at him. 'I hate reading.'

'Okay, we can read it together.'

Her face showed no response.

'Then we can discuss it and I'll help you with the assignment. How does that sound?'

She lifted her head, just a little, looking up her nose at him. 'Why don't you be nice and write it for me?'

'Be nice!' That's what you'd say to a sugar daddy. Doug felt his ire rising. Bloody insolent, he thought.

'That's not how it works.' Doug sat back in the chair and looked away from Sharna, but was aware she was still watching him, a faint smile appearing on her lips. Now her eyes were sparkling with a mischievous teasing. She didn't falter in her gaze.

'How does it work?' she asked, but it wasn't merely a question. It was a challenge. A challenge he was going to fail, one that had already tricked him into abandoning his lesson plan and left him with no room for negotiation.

You little bugger, he thought. You know you've got me a bit rattled. Well, let's call your bluff. 'They pay me to tutor here. Don't you want to study?'

'Nah!'

Douglas let his eyes drop to the book, the sense of failure irking him. He turned pages, pointlessly, avoiding looking at her. I am no match for this girl. For God's sake, she probably knows more about life than I do, stuff I only ever read in books or see in current affairs programs on the teeve.

The kind of teacher he wanted to be stirred deep inside him. Okay, he thought, you're not the only one to call a challenge. I can take a risk and call your bluff, little miss smarty-pants.

'Okay, Let's try a bit of role reversal. You be the teacher.' He held up the copy of Peter Temple's *The Broken Shore*. 'Abuse, family violence, homelessness,' he said, pointing at the book. 'Say you had to talk to a group of Year Eleven girls about these things. Where would you start, Sharna?'

The girl seemed to shrink into herself. Her face went blank, her eyes dulled and a slight tremor appeared on the rim of her upper lip, though it was so minimal Doug couldn't be sure he was seeing it. The silence closed in on them, golden silence lilting on the hum of bees gathering pollen from the plants in the side passage. Is she having a seizure or something?

The glow of the sun, the warmth in the room, the hum of bees seemed to sedate them. The girl hadn't moved, barely seemed to be breathing. Yet there was that quiver of the upper lip, which had now become more pronounced. 'Say something!' the teacher in him, the man in him, was demanding.

'Where would you start?' He knew he was being relentless, but couldn't stop himself. 'Do you know anything about that stuff?'

'Are we done here?' Her voice was hollow, but her eyes had narrowed.

Her question caught him completely off guard, unseating his attempt at older and wiser. The glint in her eyes led him back to her face. God, he thought, I've really got her offside. Quickly, recover. Do something to save the session. But his mind was blank. He'd blown it totally. This girl will never come back to tutoring.

'Up to you,' he answered dubiously.

Sharna stood up and moved to the door. She turned and looked back at him, a look so darkly ambiguous that it shocked him. He sensed with unease that she was seeing him as coming from some sad, other place where the losers lived. It was a look that clearly said that she wanted nothing to do with that place, its people or its lessons. Fuck you, class dismissed.

Doug was utterly conflicted. He resented her for getting the better of him and he blamed himself for being arrogant enough to get locked into a battle of wills with a teenager. I hurt her. It was cruel, completely unnecessary. Why did I do that?

The world had turned and the sunlight had shifted a little away from the window. In the side passage, there was more sunlight, but also shadows were lengthening, shading the tender plants from the heat of the afternoon. He needed to justify his behaviour, to analyse the lesson to work out where it had gone wrong. The whole set-up is unreasonable, he fumed. I'm supposed to teach her without any background information. That would never happen in school. If I have a problem kid, I can talk to the counsellor or the year coordinator. The bloody privacy legislation doesn't allow any information to be given about these kids. How is that supposed to work?

He felt guilty that he had wanted to shout at her, 'Don't look at me like that. You're the one without purpose, without education, facing a life of…' Of what? That girl has got under my skin, pushed the wrong buttons and…pushed buttons I should never have let her near. Aargh! He covered his face with his hands. It's not mine to judge. Leave it, he told himself.

Lifting his head, he ran his eyes over the bare walls and saw how his transgressive behaviour was inscribed in the pale paintwork, pale words with loud voices. 'You fancy her, Doug,' that's what they were saying. 'You're supposed to teach her and instead you've engaged with her emotionally. What happened to your sense of professional distance? The student-teacher relationship?'

He got up and walked around the table to the window. The tangle of grass against the fence outside heightened his awareness of his inability to unravel Sharna's obvious sense of herself as being beyond education. Where does that confidence come from? From ignorance, probably. More like over-confidence actually.

If she is to survive in the world, it's education she needs more than anything. That's how I got here. Hard bloody work. Nothing was ever handed to me on a silver platter. That's not how it works, Sharna. You've got to put in the hard yards, pull yourself out of places like this with education, application.

He crossed to the door and ran his eyes over the flourishing herbs, a sense of failure nagging at him. What the hell! I'm a teacher, not some kind of saviour. Am I blaming her for not falling for my brilliant teaching? How could she? There was no teaching, and certainly no brilliance. I've blown it.

The image of Sharna's face rose in his mind, her jewel-like eyes staring at him from above the herb pot. She's another beautiful young Aussie lost to disadvantage, poverty, probably abuse and maybe early death from drug overdose. Sharna isn't one of my middle-class school kids living at home in a family. She lives in sheltered accommodation. What makes you think that if she studied, got a matriculation, she could pull herself out of this?

His presumptions about Sharna struck home. You couldn't work an instant miracle? So? The kid just doesn't want to study. Not today, but okay, maybe next week. If she comes back, that is.

When Sharna stood up from the table, she was battling rage and contempt for the tutor. The contempt had started the moment she and Zoe walked into the study. She had recoiled inwardly at seeing the guy's eyes wander around her face. He was desperately trying not to stare at her breasts, but was unable to conceal the stolen glances. I hate guys, she thought. They're all the same, all after the same thing.

Have I read the novel? Of course I've read the novel, you dopy prick, but I'm not going to tell a perve like you. You're getting paid, so instead of ogling me, work for it. She then set out to thwart him at every turn, until his final, insinuating suggestion. Well, fuck you, pretty boy.

'Are we done here?' She was definitely done here and if he didn't like it, he could stick it. She went back to her room, pushing past Zoe on the way, and slammed her door behind her.

'What happened, Doug?' Zoe's voice snapped him out of his thoughts.

He hadn't noticed her come down to the study. He tried to clear his head, explain the failure of the lesson. He liked Zoe and she had been very welcoming to him when he arrived. We're on the same side, he thought. She'll understand.

'I'm sorry, Zoe. Sharna didn't want to work. She hasn't read the novel. Says she hates reading.' He gave a defensive chuckle. 'She wanted me to write the assignment for her.'

Zoe was nodding. 'Okay,' she said. 'Let's try again with her next week. I'll have a talk with her in the meantime. Ready for Colin?'

'Colin?' Doug had been so fixated on Sharna that he had forgotten all about a second student. At least this next one is a boy. I won't have to put up with the games. 'Okay, tell me about Colin.'

Zoe turned and walked back along the passage without answering Doug's question. 'I'll get him,' she called back.

Doug sorted through the notes he had made when the program director had discussed the tutoring with him. Colin Clarke, age sixteen. Great, Doug thought as he heard voices in the passage. I just have to work on school assignments with him. Help him to write proper English and keep him up to scratch.

'Hi, Doug, this is Colin.' Zoe waved Colin into the doorway. 'Colin, Doug is the tutor. He's good. Please work with him, hey? Give it a go.' She winked at Doug and disappeared back towards the house.

Colin's good looks took Doug by surprise. My God, what's he doing in a place like this? And Sharna? So good-looking, the two of them. His eyes flew to Colin's thick black hair, neatly cut, lustrous and crowning his head perfectly. So unlike mine, Doug thought, suddenly self-conscious about the thinning at the back of his own head. Whereas Sharna's irises were jewel boxes of precious gems, Colin's were jet-black wells of intensity with dark eyelashes like verandas protecting them. Colin's skin was as clear and unblemished as Sharna's, pale but not pasty. Her hair was an auburn blond colour, strawberry blonde he thought, soft and lustrous, while Colin's was thick and strong.

Colin was holding Doug's gaze, a bemused smile hovering around his mouth. Those lips! These kids look perfect. What's gone wrong that they end up in a residential care facility? Clearly good looks aren't a form of protection in the world they operate in. Snap out of it, man, you're freaking the kid out, staring at him like that.

'Hi, Colin. Come on in, sit down please. I'm Doug. Really happy to be working with you. Year Eleven, eh? That's huge. How are you going with it?'

Colin shrugged and sat down exactly where Sharna had been just a short while ago. The sun had moved past the window so Colin was fully in focus, not enshrined in some kind of celestial aura as Sharna had been.

As Colin sat down, two things happened simultaneously. The first was the look of intensity in his eyes changed to one of alertness. It was so charged with expectation that Doug felt immediately encouraged. Okay, he's keen to work. That's good. He smiled and nodded at Colin, but as he did so a predation came into Colin's look that struck Doug forcibly. He had to look away.

The second thing was that Colin began rubbing his crotch. Doug's eyes went to the boy's groin. Colin stared down Doug's sense of embarrassment. Don't know what that's all about, but I'm going to ignore it. Doug drew in a breath, sat back in his chair and cleared his throat. Even so, his eyes kept wanting to look down at Colin's crotch and the rubbing which had now become more like a scratching.

'Okay,' Doug said a little too loudly. 'Pull in your chair and let's see what you have here.' He picked up an assignment sheet that the boy had put on the table and forced his eyes to read it. A Midsummer Night's Dream, eh. Great play. Have you read it? No? Seen it?'

Colin didn't pull his chair in. He didn't want to talk about the play or the assignment. He didn't want to talk about schoolwork at all.

What he was interested in was Doug, his work as a teacher, the kids in his school and he fired questions as Doug tried to pull the attention back to the assignment.

'You married?' Colin suddenly asked during a bout of scratching his balls.

Doug wasn't sure whether to answer or not. 'No, not married.'

'That figures. Thought not. Girlfriend?' Scratch, scratch, grin, rub, rub, crotch, eyes on Doug, grin.

Doug knew he had to get off this train of talk just as he had to get his eyes off Colin's groin. But he couldn't help himself meeting the challenge head on. 'What do you mean "that figures"?'

A look of mischief came into those dark wells hiding under the veranda lashes and Colin's lips parted in what Doug could only decide was a suggestive smile. 'You're a young guy. You're good-looking, look very fit, work-out type. You'll be sleeping around, getting as much as you can.' Scratch, rub, massage.

He's got an erection? For God's sake! I've had enough. 'Can you stop that?'

'I'm itchy. You can help.'

'What?' That can't mean what I think it does. Doug's eyes wouldn't obey him and kept looking at Colin's crotch. Zoe, he thought. Get Zoe. He started to rise from the table and as he turned, he saw Zoe hovering in the passage. He realised she had been listening to what was being said in the study.

Doug had a crushing feeling that he had been caught out doing something wrong. He felt a weird kind of guilt about the boy opposite, about the scratching, the touching of his private parts so openly in front of him. He felt as if it was he who had been touching Colin and Zoe had caught him at it. 'I don't touch students!' he wanted to yell. 'I'm not a pedo!' That term of abuse that students at school used against teachers they didn't like.

Zoe stepped into the doorway. She had an enigmatic smile on her face, which confused Doug even more than he already was.

'Can I have a word with you?' Doug managed to get out.

Once in the passageway, Doug felt a modicum of command come back. He steered Zoe up the passage towards the open door of the lounge room. 'Zoe, what's going on with Colin? I mean, he keeps touching himself, scratching his crotch, rubbing his… Right in front of me. Is he coming on to me or something?'

Zoe was nodding. 'Sorry about that. Don't know about the come on. I wouldn't put it past him. But he's scratching because he's got crabs.'

'What!' Doug stared at her as the spectre of a legion of lice marching across the desk from Colin's body to his overcame him. He immediately felt the urge to scratch. 'You mean scabies?'

She nodded.

'But there're treatments for that. You don't need a prescription. You can get the stuff over the counter.'

'He knows that.'

Zoe's apparent lack of concern flabbergasted Doug. The kid's suffering. All that scratching – his skin will end up raw, bleeding maybe, infected where the lice get into the wounds. He shook his head at the grossness of it. 'Can I take him to the chemist? Maybe he's embarrassed to front up himself and buy the stuff? Does he have money?'

'Colin embarrassed?' Zoe laughed, 'I don't think so.' She was shaking her head. 'No, don't do that. Colin knows what to do. He chooses not to go and buy the medication. If he wants to live with the irritation, that's his decision.'

Wow, Doug thought, that's really tough love. In the meantime, I'm supposed to get him concentrating on Year Eleven. He sits there scratching and staring and I sit here wondering if I'm going to get crabs from him. How are we going to pass paper to each other? Pens? The Shakespeare text? Doug's imagination conjured a Forest of Arden crawling with scabies rather than fairies. Helena and Hermia scratching away at themselves while they squabbled, Demetrius and Lysander rolling down their tights and squashing the little bastards with their thumbnails. He shook his head. Zoe was watching him. She raised a quizzical eyebrow. Doug nodded curtly and walked back to the study.

'Okay, Colin, let's look at this assignment and see if…'

'Do you want to see them?' Colin was grinning at him, stroking his groin. 'They're all over my pubes.'

Doug started reading the assignment task out loud.

Colin stretched back in his chair, both hands cupped over his genitals and smiled at Doug. 'You're a real cutie.'

'Stop it, Colin. I'm not interested in any of that. What I want to do is help you get back into studying. You've got a high IQ and it's an awful shame to waste that.'

For the next half-hour, Doug tried to work on the assignment, but he eventually gave up having done most of the talking and prompting while Colin gave monosyllabic answers that did not indicate any comprehension of the task at hand.

When the session was over, Colin left the study with a peremptory 'See ya' and Doug was left alone wondering what he was supposed to do.

'I can't do this,' he said to Zoe when they were alone in the lounge room. 'Sharna's level of disengagement is bad enough, but Colin…' He paused, rewinding the scene in the study over in his mind. He shook his head again. 'I feel totally inadequate. I'd be taking money under false pretences.'

'Don't worry,' she said. 'It was a good start.'

Doug snorted. 'You're kidding!'

'No, I'm not. They stayed for most of the lesson. That's better than we've had in the past with other tutors. She looked at him and went on. 'These kids are very damaged. Don't be fooled by their appearance. Underneath the good looks, neat clothes, the apparent control is a seething mass of very, very personal issues. You've done well. Let's see how it goes next week, okay?'

The next week, Doug turned up on time and full of resolution to break through with at least one of them.

'Sharna ready?' he asked.

'Sorry,' Zoe answered. She's gone to get her rent money.'

'Will she be long? I mean, has she gone to the ATM up at the shops?'

Zoe's look was a mixture of apology and practicality. 'She's gone to earn it. That could take a while. Depends on how many clients she gets.'

Doug stared at Zoe as the meaning of what she had just said sank in. 'You mean… I mean, are we talking prostitution here?'

She nodded. 'Sex work? Yes. Afraid so. Don't know where Colin is. He owes us for rent too. Let's have a cuppa and you can tell me a bit more about yourself while we wait.'

Back in the high school between sessions at the residential unit, Doug felt oddly attached to his ragtag group of students. He couldn't imagine any of them living lives like Sharna and Colin, but was now acutely aware how little he knew about their private lives. Teachers don't know what goes on in their homes each morning before school, whether there have been fights with siblings, whether they have been shouted at by parents, hit or whether they are suffering worse kinds of abuse.

When he was on playground duty during the week, Doug was impressed by the way the hundreds of kids managed the altercations over handball and soccer without much intervention from him other than 'Pick it up and put it in the bin', or 'What are you guys doing around here? You know this area is out of bounds.'

Could any of these kids end up in a care facility? The thought made him reflect on his relationship with his students. He knew he was good at teaching the curriculum, good at classroom discipline, good at monitoring each student's progress. What he had to admit was that he took little notice of the pastoral care of them. Not only that, he didn't know how to do it, didn't know what it involved. Doug determined to ask around and get a discussion going amongst the staff about it.

There's so much that affects the lives of these kids and I don't know a thing about it. So much of it is none of my business. I guess we just

have to take them at face value and teach them to think for themselves
as best we can.

Doug decided that it was in the school that he really wanted to
make a difference. He rang the director and told her he couldn't work
at the residential facility, that it was a worthy cause, but he wanted to
put all his energy into teaching at school.

Over the next couple of years, Doug thought often and deeply about
that short time at the residential facility. He carried a sense of failure
that he had given up, had not been able to do some learning with Sharna and Colin. Every child is capable of learning, he believed. A teacher
just has to find the right approach to make it work for the kid.

He often wondered what had happened to Sharna and Colin. A
clue came one morning in the city. He was heading for a curriculum
meeting with the Department of School Education and had ducked
into a café across the road for a takeaway coffee. Standing at the back
of the crowd, he took in the people waiting to be served. There were
the usual office workers, a couple of road workers and a well-dressed
and groomed young woman.

There was something about the young woman's hair that stirred a
distant memory, but he couldn't put his finger on what it was. His eyes
were drawn to her shoes, which looked very expensive. As he looked
up, the young woman turned to look behind her. Their eyes locked.
He never understood how she managed to register non-recognition and
recognition at the same time. Neither of them acknowledged the other,
but Doug knew that the young woman was Sharna. Their eyes drifted
off each other and the moment was over.

Sitting at the big table in the department, staring into his coffee
while the arguments went back and forth as to what should be in and
what should be out of the new syllabus, Doug surmised with a fair
degree of certainty that Sharna at eighteen or nineteen was a successful
sex worker who could afford expensive shoes and to have her hair perfectly styled. She had found her niche and he was forgotten, as incon-
sequential to her life as a disposable takeaway coffee cup.

When Jesus was a Blond

Johnny lay back on his beach towel, soaking up the sun. He was completely stoned. Every part of his body was suffused with desire and contentment. He was at one with his golden beach world, wrapped all over with its azure covering stretched high above him. The surf rolling in sang of seafarers adventuring across deep waters crested with the white foam of mermaids and mermen diving under the sailors' barques. Pirate adventures, South Sea paradises and Spanish galleons carrying Inca and Aztec gold to Madrid swam across the expanded breadth of his mind.

God, I love the sun, he mused. I love God and the sun. I bet Jesus used to strip down to the waist when he was carpentering with his dad. Out there in the yard sawing away at timber for the Roman overlords, getting a golden tan at the same time. I prefer this way of doing it, he giggled, running his hand over his taut, flat belly, feeling the heat of his skin, thinking of diving back into the surf, frolicking with the merpeople.

Did Jesus ever smoke weed? No! But I reckon Jesus might have been the first surfie. He would have stood on the shore of the Sea of Galilee and watched the waves roll in. Were there waves on the Sea of Galilee? Sure, there were.

There would have been planks of wood from all those shipwrecks washing up in the surf. I reckon he would have worked out that if you could stand on a plank, you could then ride it into shore. He was a carpenter, okay? And the Son of God! So he would have experimented with planks, cutting them, shaping them, sanding them and getting the right balance.

His father probably cracked a mental about him wasting time on surfboards when there was so much work to be done for the Romans and the rich Greeks and Judeans. But that's how dads are. A guy like Jesus would have done more than his fair share of the hard work.

The big surfboard breakthrough would have been the fin. But hey, he was Jesus and he probably knew intuitively that that's what was needed – a bit like a keel on a trireme.

'Jesus wants me for a sunbeam.' The words sang in his head, rolling over and over with the breakers hitting the shoreline. I don't want to be a sunbeam. I want to be a surfie, like Jesus, blond with all that sun like me.

In Jesus's time, the world was Roman. The Romans weren't beach people. They didn't surf, didn't sunbake and didn't go to surf-club dances. They busied themselves conquering the world and cutting down most of the trees around the Mediterranean to build ships, temples, houses, stuff like that. I guess it kept Jesus and his dad in work. Oh yes, and they governed. That's why they went around conquering the world, so they could tell people what to do. Just like Dad does.

Since then, others have tried to copy the Romans, Johnny reflected, digging up vague memories from Year Eight and Year Nine history and info picked up from docos on the TV. Charlemagne, the Holy Roman Empire, Ferdinand and Isabella, the British empire, the Ottoman empire and the French under Napoleon. None of them were surfing societies – which was more the pity, he told himself. There might have been more skin cancer in the world, but there would have been less violence.

It would be great to still be wearing togas, or those short, sexy tunics the Roman guys wear in the movies.

He lay there, somnolent, absorbing the sun's rays without any sense of guilt at the burning sensation, but luxuriating in the belief that tanned and blond was beautiful. It amused him to think of Jesus on a surfboard, wet, blond locks flying out behind him as he hung five on a two-metre wave off the coast of Judea. The vision of all those gorgeous Hebrew chicks sitting on the sand dunes, knees hitched under their chins, watching adoringly as Jesus swung off the wave, turned the board round and paddled back out to sea. That could be me, Johnny thought. Would that be blasphemy? He sighed and let the blasphemous train of thoughts sink under a perfectly formed, incoming wave.

Would I like to have been Roman or Galilean? The Romans had the power, but you would have had to work too hard to maintain it. Besides, they crucified Jesus, the bastards. That was a great loss: probably set surfing back a couple of thousand years.

My blond and Catholic family came into existence two thousand years after Rome. Blond was the norm as I was growing up in a Sydney beachside suburb. All the world was blond and it was normal and beautiful. I knew nothing about Anglo-Saxon or Anglo-Celtic genes and wouldn't have cared even if I had.

An image of his family flitted into his mind. It was so vivid he knew he was remembering them from real life. After all, he had been with them that morning, at Mass and at breakfast before trotting down to the beach. That had been just over an hour ago.

He lifted his head and looked at the waves. Beautiful! Should have brought my board. Damn. He lay back and stretched out on his towel, letting the image of his family return.

My mother is light honey blonde and my father is one of those blond Irish boys with periwinkle blue eyes. My brother's hair is so blonde it is almost white. My sister has honey-blonde hair like me, though hers is paler than mine. In summer, the family turns even blonder as we swim and sunbake our way into skin cancers… Johnny tutted and dismissed the cancer thought in irritation as an unwelcome intrusion on his musings.

I regard blond hair as a direct gift from Jesus. It is his way of calling us to come unto him and be in the blond community. I'm sure that doesn't mean I need to get into carpentry or any other physical work, though. This is good as I am pretty bad with saws, hammers and nails. Very un-Jesus-like! Once I built a set of shelves for the laundry at home and smashed my thumb with the hammer. This would never have happened had I been true to form and spent the morning on the beach rather than trying to ingratiate myself with my mother.

When I was younger, it never occurred to me to question being blond. Everyone around us seemed to be blond in a way, within a range of hair colours from mousy to brunette to pale white. Even if people I liked didn't have blond hair, I think I somehow squeezed them into the blond range. That meant I lived in a hegemonic blond-dom. To be was to be blond. Descartes got it wrong. After all, on the beaches where blond reigned supreme along with surfing, beach blond became elevated to the status of national identity.

Though it never occurred to me to think about the ethnic demographic of the suburb we lived in, I was aware that our neighbourhood was solidly Irish Catholic. There were plenty of Protestants around, but that was all right because as children we played with them in the back lane during the week and prayed for their conversion in church on Sunday. I giggled at the absurdity of it.

All the holy pictures show Jesus with long dark hair. As a kid, I knew that couldn't be right because that would make him a Protestant or Italian. No, Jesus must have been blond, so I squeezed him into the blonde normal range. Sometimes, I would hold a holy picture in a way so that the light fell on it and turned Jesus's dark hair into light brunette. That's how it should be.

Only the Italian husband of one of my mother's friends was a counterpoint to a world of blond. Not that he made me think about our blondness. Rather it made me think about Italian black hair. Without questioning the blondness of the world, Bruno's glossy, Italian black hair made him different, not the norm, an oddity in complete contrast to us and the red hair and pale freckled skin of his Australian wife. At the time, in my mind, the handsome Bruno with the beautiful, smooth singing voice was a statistical deviation even if Surry Hills, where he lived, wasn't the limits of the known world. Jesus would be all right about Bruno and forgive him his black hair.

The turning point came for me a couple of years ago. The first knockout realisation of blond banality came crashing in when I looked at a coloured photograph, taken on a little Brownie box camera. Someone, a parent, friend, schoolmate, who knows, took a photo of me and my brother and sister, sitting side by side on our towels on the sand at an unidentified beach. This was really unusual as my brother and I didn't get on all that well. There was nothing odd about us being on a beach, of course. We spent a lot of time on beaches up and down the Sydney coastline. Lean, blonde, blue-eyed, my sister in a two-piece and my brother and I in hip-hugging Speedos, and beautifully tanned.

It was an ordinary enough photograph, much like the myriad other badly composed and poorly lit snapshots that only a Brownie box camera could achieve. The thing about this photo was that the three of us look like Hitler youth. The close-cropped blond hair, the blue eyes with hard, cold stares, the strong jutting jaw-lines and the tensed bodies looking ready to spring to attention at the merest murmur of an 'Achtung!' bored into me as I looked at it.

Nazis were like the Romans, barging around conquering the world, bullying people into submission and they definitely were not into surfing. But their ideal was Aryan blond, and there we were exemplifying that ideal. So where does that leave my blond Jesus? He wouldn't have been a Nazi, that's for sure. The more I think about it, the more I don't want to be that Aryan-looking boy in the photo.

Johnny sat up. He needed to look at the surf to clear his mind. No Nazis out there, he thought, and if there are, the only things to conquer are the waves. Hmm! I ought to grow my hair long. Nazis didn't have long hair.

Johnny dismissed the Nazis from this mind and lay back on his towel. Why did we look so cranky in that snapshot? The more closely I had studied it, the more inclined I was to believe that the photo had been posed. We three unwilling children had been corralled onto the beach towels, told to relax, look out to sea and not notice the camera. My sister and I are, of course, looking directly at the photographer while my brother has turned his surly expression on some poor innocent nearby.

Johnny rolled onto his front, turning his back to the sun. What's more, sunbathers don't line up in a neat row on their towels. They usually sprawl over an area of sand, taking up more room than they need.

Sometimes, they lie facing each other so they can talk, or position themselves to catch the full rays of the sun. He lifted his head just enough to look around, checking that that was right, then snuggled down into the towel luxuriating in the warmth of those rays.

Occasionally, he mused on, some crafty bugger sits down in a place where they can steal secret glances at someone close by who has taken their fancy, or simply to gaze at the surf and surfers. He giggled at the perviness of it.

So why was this snapshot of us three reluctant children taken? Was it intended as a portrait of children in their near-naked youthfulness? He turned over and rested on his elbows, looking down his body, taking in the narrow strip of nylon stretched across his pelvis. He grinned at the bulge in the apex of his legs then frowned as a new thought struck him. Near-naked youthfulness, eh! That would be very concerning. Or maybe it was someone's attempt to capture the Nordic blondness of three adolescent Australian children so conspicuously displaying their genetic heritage, as my mother calls it.

Johnny mulled over his mother's insistence that she was the illegitimate daughter of her mother and a Norwegian journalist who was working in Sydney in the early part of the twentieth century. What on earth would a Norwegian journalist be doing in Sydney at that time? How many Norwegians even knew that Australia existed? Then again, he thought, if there was even a gleam of truth in Mum's claim, it would help explain the blondness. As everyone knows – that is, my mother knows – all Norwegians are blond.

Did she ever consider her husband's, my father's, Irishness might have played a part in our looks?

This Aryan stuff doesn't leave much room for blond Jesus as the prototype of perfect blond-dom, Johnny concluded. Jesus definitely was not Scandinavian or German. It's not rocket science, he chuckled softly: Jesus was Galilean, a Jew, but still perfectly blond and a surfie.

As these thoughts drifted through his mind, he was distracted by a young mother nearby, battling to get her little kids to sit still on a towel so she could take a picture of them with the surf in the background.

That's it! Johnny patted his thighs in triumph. All snapshots are posed. Just think how much the imagery of Jesus over the centuries was posed. There was the tall, strong Jesus, the gentle Jesus meek and mild, the all-merciful and forgiving Jesus and the sorrowing Jesus in the garden of Gethsemane. Then those Italian painters in the Renaissance were determined to give him dark Italian hair. Not one portrait of him as a surfie. Now he is depicted as African, South American Indian, Chinese – everybody has had a go and they've all got it wrong. So what was he really like?

He yawned.

Johnny looked around. A lot more people had arrived at the beach. There and there and that one – dark-haired, brunettes, redheads and the black-haired, they're everywhere. I'm surrounded by them. Dark hair must have been in existence since way before I was born. He closed his eyes. The bright sun burning over his lids projected images of Jesus turning dark-haired in the holy pictures, in the painted statuary and in the religious books. It's an unproclaimed miracle he chuckled. I am the only person alive to bear witness to it. Halleluiah!

Okay, Jesus was probably not a blond surfie. But that's all right because if he returns to earth in the Second Coming and arrives at the beach, even his hair will turn blondish from the surf and sun. I can imagine him riding a surfboard, wearing board shorts and eating fish and chips on the sand. After all, he was the friend of fishermen back in the day so would have been familiar with fish lunches by the Sea of Galilee. Though I don't know what he will think of the deep-fried batter.

'God, it's hot,' Johnny said out loud as he stood up.

A woman lying on her front looked up at him and nodded. I wasn't talking to you, he smiled. I was talking to Jesus, the Son of God. The woman smiled back at him.

Time for a swim. Good-looking waves out there. Wouldn't it be great if Jesus cruised by and we went bodysurfing together?

I wonder what he's up to?

Terms of Love and Loss

'I've missed you so much. I know it's only been two weeks since I moved here, but it seems an eternity.' Daniel smiled at Suzie. 'You look fantastic, blooming.' He was examining her closely. 'Has me not being around done that?' he laughed.

'I have something to tell you,' she said in a low voice.

'Isn't this place great?' Daniel grinned at her, nodding to the park outside the big plate-glass windows. 'Sydney is so beautiful.' He took her hand. 'You are so beautiful. Why don't you move here, too? We could get a place together.'

Suzie withdrew her hand from his. Did he hear what I said? she wondered, turning away to look out the windows.

Beyond the glass walls of the restaurant on this late Sunday in March, Centennial Park wore an autumnal green, brought on by showers earlier in the week. Kids, revved up with full bellies and impatient at having to sit while the adults finished their meals, were now running around outside while their parents sipped coffee and chatted.

Suzie had flown to Sydney on Friday evening to present workshops and talks over the weekend at the New South Wales English Teachers' Association annual conference. Daniel had booked a table for Sunday lunch at the café in Centennial Park. It was the only free time she had as she was flying back to Melbourne later that evening.

This has to be done face-to-face, she had finally decided. I can't go back to Melbourne and email or text him.

Neither had quite expected the café to be so full and it was only now, after they had eaten and the café had started emptying that Suzie felt able to say what she wanted.

Daniel felt panic grip him at Suzie's words. 'Pregnant!'

Suzie nodded. Her hand strayed across the table and she laid it on his arm. His face was an open book but kept returning to the one questioning frown.

She cut him off before he could ask. 'It's yours. Ours. There's no other possibility.'

The waiter put coffee cups on the table and a dish of four small, sweet pastilles. Daniel stared at the pattern the barista had made in the froth on top of his latte. A tree sprouting leaves. New life.

He looked up at Suzie. 'A baby? I thought you…'

She covered her eyes. 'Oh God! I went off the pill. You were using condoms and I thought that was enough. I wanted a break from contraception, from the responsibility. Then you were having trouble. I went back on the pill when we thought if you didn't have to put on a condom, things would start working again. But it wasn't that simple, was it? So I stopped taking it again. Then we had sex. Wonderful sex and…'

Daniel was shaking his head. 'Suzie, Suzie.'

'I know, I know. Please don't blame me. You said you were sure of…'

'Of being heterosexual.'

There was a pause while they looked into each other's eyes, looking for different answers.

Daniel's face coloured, remembering . Did I lie to her when I said that? I meant it at the time, I believed I could be straight, but it wasn't true. There's a vast difference between wanting to be and actually being something.

He glanced across at her sitting upright, lost in her own thoughts. I love her. Why is the sex a problem for me? I want her, I just can't perform.

Straight/gay, it matters. I thought I wanted to be straight, to be like other boys, like Aaron, my best mate, he reflected. In fact, he had competed with Aaron for Suzie and had won to the extent that he and Suzie had got together. Daniel wasn't sure if Aaron knew how involved they had become.

But I'm not like him, he admitted. I know I'm not because the boys

I really wanted to be like were the boys I had been having sex with since I was seventeen. I knew all that at the time, but still convinced myself that with Suzie I had become heterosexual. It would have been so much easier if only I had known, if there had been someone to tell me at the time that at a long stretch, I am bisexual. Back then, I didn't even know the word, let alone what it meant.

'Am I sure of being heterosexual? Being straight?' He turned away from her, and watched the kids playing outside. Kids, oh God! He turned back to her. 'I thought I was.'

'Thought, not sure?' she murmured. Her words hung between them over the coffee and jelly pastilles separating them on the table. 'Not sure,' she mouthed.

Daniel winced at the tumult of emotions welling up in him as the impact of his indecision, his ambivalence, struck him with nauseating force. 'I have betrayed you,' he whispered, 'totally compromised you.'

There was a burst of laughter from the parents at the nearby table. To Daniel, the sound had a mocking quality, an indictment of him. I'm gutless. What did I think I was doing? Playing at being Aaron? He glanced at the men and women at the next table, at the smiles on their faces, at their assured sexuality. I could never be like that.

He took her hand that had stayed on his arm and put it to his lips. He gently kissed the fingers. 'I'm so, so sorry.'

She eased her hand out of his, turning her eyes towards the park. She flicked a finger across her cheek.

Is she crying? I'm crazy letting go of her. She is so beautiful, so clever, so much my perfect woman. I just can't make love to her. And that's insurmountable.

A golden hue from the park suffused the restaurant, giving it an other-worldly ambiance. For an instant, Daniel saw the couples, the tables and chairs float above the wooden floor and he was elevating with them. His body felt completely emptied of heaviness. Then he blinked and the illusion dissipated.

Pregnant! Me a father? God, I'm only twenty. She's older than me, she'll know what to do. I'll have to marry her. Husband and wife! No, I can't. How can we be man and wife if I can't be a husband, be a man for her? Dad, Daddy. Oh God!

They were silent as the aromatic coffee wafted their thoughts backwards and forwards, offering no answers.

Suzie suddenly stirred her cup. 'Aaron asked me to marry him.'

'What?' Daniel blurted it out. He was aghast at the prospect of being superseded by his best mate. It's my child, my baby. 'Marry him? Does he know? About the baby?'

Aaron was besotted with Suzie. He had taken her out almost as often as Daniel had himself. They'd had words about her, and a tense rivalry had developed.

Aaron had told Daniel to back off, leave Suzie to him. 'You're gay, mate. Guys, that's your thing. Leave the girl to me.'

Were those words the thing that incited me to think I could be a proper lover to Suzie? Did Aaron's bullying spur me on to put my sexuality to the test with her?

Then another thought, but one that he had had to consider many times in the past, occurred to him. Aaron! The all-Aussie male! Aaron, best mate since primary school, joint conspirator in making mischief around the neighbourhood, fellow team member in the local footy club – was there some perverse way I substituted Suzie for Aaron? That's so fucked, but not beyond the realms of possibility. Jesus!

No! A shattering thought crashed into Daniel's mind. No, he screamed inside, no, no! He sat up and stared at her. 'You've been sleeping with him, haven't you? With Aaron?'

She looked down into the drained coffee cup. Her hair hung down, covering her face. She was still, silent, unreadable.

Daniel closed his eyes. She has. She's been sleeping with both of us. The idea both thrilled and angered him. Me and Aaron, both having sex with her. It's almost like having sex with him by proxy.

He opened his eyes, but she kept her head down, her hair hanging loose. 'Suzie, does Aaron know you're pregnant?' he asked again.

She shook her head. Then she sat up, her wide eyes defiant, boring into him.

'What makes you so sure it's not his? I mean, if you've been sleeping with both of us…'

'Have no doubt about that. Aaron always wore a condom, always.' She drew in a deep breath, but her jaw was set and her face was tense. 'I've only just found out I'm pregnant.' Her face softened. 'I think it happened the night before you left. Our break-up sex night.'

'But you had gone off the pill. On, off. What were you thinking?'

She was shaking her head from side to side. 'Neither of us was thinking that night.'

'You could terminate it.' He realised how confronting what he had just blurted out was, but it was out there and it was too late to retract it.

Suzie didn't answer. She turned her eyes to the park, avoiding the brutal possibility of an abortion. Two mounted policemen, both only a little older than she and Daniel, were passing by on their horses. They had stopped as the kids ran up to the guard rail to look at the horses. They were talking to the kids, smiling and patting the necks of their mounts. The sight changed Suzie's mood to one of sentimentality, a sense of becoming a part of that wider world of family.

The rangers looked so handsome. Tight britches hugged the strong thighs, tan boots almost to the knees. Muscly arms, large hands lightly holding the reins. She noticed the thick brown hair of the nearer rider curling below his helmet. The confidence of the two men, their straight backs, the magnificent poise of the horses came together as a powerful image, an amalgam of mythical centaurs and masculine virility. I'm sexualising them she thought. It's hormonal. No, they're just two young guys doing a job. Time and a half for weekend work. But they are sexy, too. I don't want to live without sex. And I want this baby, Daniel's baby.

Daniel had followed her gaze and was staring at the rangers. Her breath caught in her chest. He'd rather go to bed with them than with me. But I'm the one carrying his child. She looked away from him and put her hands to her mouth, stifling a low sob. The action drew

Daniel's eyes back to her. I love him and he loves me, but it's not that simple.

'What are we going to do?'

His question was as much an inner reflection as one addressed to her. It had been careering around in her head ever since the pregnancy had been confirmed.

She took his hands. There was fear in him, she could almost smell its animal tang. He'll marry me if I ask him, but it would destroy both of us in the end. I couldn't bear it if we started hating each other. Terminate? I don't want that, though maybe it's the rational thing to do under the circumstances.

The waiter stood beside them with the bill.

'Oh,' she said to Daniel, 'you didn't drink your coffee. It will be cold. Can I get you a fresh one?'

Daniel shook his head. Suzie took out a credit card and paid the bill. They stood up, bewildered eyes looking into each other. Not knowing what the future held for them, they embraced impulsively, holding each other tightly, feeling their hearts beating to very different rhythms.

Suzie burst into tears. Daniel led her out of the restaurant excoriated by the frowns, hostile looks and tut-tutting of the other patrons and staff. They walked in silence to a small copse and she let him hold her as she wept. It was all he could do as the sense of guilt and the feeling of hopelessness combined to push him to the brink of despair.

'Suzie, I know you're angry with me, but I don't know how to get us out of this predicament we're in.'

'It's not a fucking predicament!' she shouted. 'It's a baby. Your baby.'

Growing up, Daniel had always assumed that one day he would be a father, have his own family. It wasn't something he ever questioned. Not even as his sexuality came roaring in and bowled him over. Yet as he stood there under the trees, the truth was that in one sense he was about to become a father and, in another sense, not. He was too young to properly comprehend it, too frightened to deal with it and too gutless to admit that he didn't want it.

All Daniel had to offer was a shoulder for Suzie to cry on while he gazed at the dark green stand of trees on the other side of the grassy sward. He kept asking her to marry him, but he could only do it in his head. He couldn't say the words out loud. It was like doing the right thing by her while doing nothing at all. So he held her and gazed at the trees in the distance, listening to the fluttering of his heart. Gutless, it intoned.

Nonetheless, Daniel was devastated when a week later, Suzie rang and told him that she had decided to go ahead with the pregnancy. I must be mad to think she'd terminate it, he inwardly groaned. I've never known Suzie to shirk her responsibility. Not like me.

Daniel stoically followed the unfolding events from Sydney as Suzie entered on a whirlwind affair with Aaron. Aaron never said anything directly about his winning Suzie from Daniel. However, Daniel perceived an unspoken sense of triumph in Aaron that left him nursing his wounded pride, though the feeling went hand in hand with an immense sense of release.

The final thrust of shame came when Suzie accepted Aaron's proposal of marriage. She extracted a promise from Daniel that he would forgo any claim of paternity over the child. Daniel had agreed even though he was completely conflicted over the rights and wrongs of his decision.

'I want this baby to have a father,' she had argued. 'If you can't be the father, then Aaron can.'

Suzie's single-minded determination silenced Daniel. Forgoing acknowledgement of paternity was a kick in the guts that left Daniel emotionally crippled. But he knew that Aaron would never go ahead with the marriage if he thought the baby wasn't his…especially if he thought it was Daniel's. He had no option but to follow Suzie's wishes.

'The baby might as well be his under the circumstances,' Suzie suggested, but they both knew that the argument was feeble, pathetic really.

Even worse was the nagging realisation that he was complicit in something that was totally wrong. He and Suzie were duping Aaron, tricking him over something as fundamental as the paternity of this baby. He was tormented day and night by the question, how can I do this to my best mate, to Aaron of all people?

He turned his accusations on Suzie. How can she have sex with Aaron knowing that the baby in her womb is mine? When she is with him, is she thinking of me?

Daniel was riven by jealousy. He argued with Suzie, but she always came back at him saying that what she was doing was best for all of them. It was morally outrageous, but there weren't alternatives. She knew Daniel couldn't guarantee that he would stay with her, that he wouldn't stray.

Daniel used every form of social media, phone calls and Zoom to keep in touch with Suzie about her affair with Aaron. He also frequently called Aaron and they talked and laughed and joked about what Aaron called his 'courtship' of Suzie. Daniel was gutted by these conversations, but he couldn't stop contacting them. He was aroused at the sound of their voices and in each's reflections on the other. He yearned to be a part of their love, but knew that in a way he was losing the two loves of his life.

It was Suzie describing how passionate Aaron was that ignited in Daniel a sexual passion for his mate that had probably been dormant since primary school. It wasn't so much sex with Aaron by proxy any more, but more a voyeuristic fascination with imagining his mate and Suzie making love.

The undeniable upside of the situation was that with Aaron, Suzie could have a satisfying family life and follow her career. And so Daniel resigned himself to becoming a sort-of uncle to his little son. And they would all live a lie.

When Aaron asked him to be his best man at the wedding, Daniel decided to move back to Melbourne. He regretted leaving Sydney just as he was settling into it, but reserved at the back of his mind the notion that he would return one day and live there.

The images of the wedding screened in Daniel's memory often. His life was riven with remorse verging on guilt at the image of himself as best man, standing beside his best mate, his secret love, knowing that the woman standing beside Aaron was the other secret love of his life and that she was carrying his child.

Daniel never knew whether Aaron guessed the truth of his marriage, the truth of his best mate's loyalty to the family and his devotion to the little boy who was born. Sometimes, Daniel would see Aaron staring at him as he played with little James. Daniel would grin at Aaron and his heart would flip whenever this was greeted by a smile and a wink.

Daniel's love for Suzie didn't wane after the marriage and birth. In truth, it grew stronger as he watched her being a mother. The sense of regret that had been so painful at the time of the wedding settled into a place in his heart where it was like an old scar that only sometimes itched. But it was this scar that always undermined any possible long-term relationship for him.

He was fortified by his love for his son and his love for Suzie and Aaron. That hidden scar of regret usually surfaced around James' birthdays and that was the time when he most wanted to cry, 'Hey, James, I'm your father, your real father.'

But he never said it, and the boy never knew the truth.

Perfectly Imperfect

A different love that dares to speak its name.

The board was shocked. Carey had told them he was resigning as artistic director of the disability theatre project. Surely they had seen this coming.

'The fact is I need time out. I'll be leaving at the end of the year.' He paused, taken aback by the stunned silence in the room. More explanation, he wondered? Say something, anything. 'I've enjoyed making those shows with the members. I think they got a lot out of it. I know I did.' Stop raving. Suck up to them. 'And I really appreciate the support that you as a board have given me over the past five years. But now I need time out to think where I'm going in the arts. You know.' They don't know. They haven't a clue why I'm doing this. 'Check out other independent theatre groups, see what they are up to. I'm taking some time off work. Then I'll see what I want to do.'

He handed a piece of paper to the president. 'You have a few months to look for a replacement director if you start now. I've jotted down the names of some drama practitioners who have worked with people with disability. They're all keen to work with this company.'

The final session with the drama group members was very emotional. Carey promised to keep in touch and come to their shows. Everyone wished everyone Merry Christmas. There were hugs and some tears and then it was over. He got into his car and drove down the highway to his home, Yolanda his partner, and the summer break ahead.

Carey and Yolanda had avoided the conflicts over which family to spend Christmas with by booking a site in a camping ground down the south coast. They deliberately chose a small rocky bay with a strip of white sand between the folds of the two points. It was less popular than other places and they hoped it would be less crowded. In fact, the site was booked to capacity, but since it was a small camping ground compared to others, it would be comfortable enough for them.

When they arrived, they set up their tent, introduced themselves to their neighbours and settled down for three weeks of hiking, surfing in the ocean and swimming in the lagoon. They concocted amazing meals out of what they had brought with them, went to a local co-op to buy fresh fish and seafood and made love whenever and wherever they could. On most nights, they had drinks with other campers, mostly families, and enjoyed the stories told around the campfire.

The kids in the camp loved Carey. Even the adolescents put aside their attitude and competed with the little kids for time with him on the beach and around campfires. 'You'll make a perfect father one day,' one of the mothers told him over drinks and the others agreed. Sometimes, it took all Yolanda's ingenuity to get Carey away from the fan club, but she was persistent and he was willing, so they did manage a lot of time to themselves in the surrounding bush and along the coastline.

'God, I don't want kids!' Carey yelled across the scrub as he relieved himself against a twisted melaleuca. They had extricated themselves from the campsite after lunch on Christmas Eve, and were walking a track they hadn't been on before. He had been in demand all morning from the kids wanting him to surf with them, from the adults needing help with setting up the fire pits for turkey, ham, roast vegetables and pudding.

'What's with the traditional English Christmas on a beach? I don't get it.' Carey called to Yolanda. 'Why can't we just have a barbecue?'

'I don't know,' she grinned, admiring the lack of inhibition and the ease with which he could stand there, pull down his shorts and urinate. Not a care in the world, that's Carey. Well, that's Carey on holiday. He's been incredibly responsible, caring and sensitive with the guys in the theatre company over the last few years. He's got it in him to be a great dad, but there's a reluctance… What is it? Selfishness? Is that it?

'The mothers reckon you'll make the perfect father,' she went on, then laughed. 'You certainly seem to like kids.'

'So long as they're not mine.'

'Having kids is not like having all those munchkins at the same time,' Yolanda scoffed.

She moved off along the track, her mind on the issues around children for them. We've never talked about it, she thought. If I am going to have kids, Carey is the perfect man for me. She had been thinking about having a baby for some time – if she was to have children, she wanted them while she was still under thirty. But would she have babies if he was against it?

He was calling to her, pointing out something he had seen. He's such a free agent, she thought, that's why he doesn't want to be tied down with babies. How serious is he when he says he doesn't want kids? We ought to have that conversation soon. If it's going to happen, Carey has to be totally on board with it.

'What's put a smile on your face?' he asked as he caught up with her and put his arms around her waist.

'Kids,' she said. 'You know, having kids of our own.'

'As I just said,' he laughed, 'I don't want kids.' He looked at Yolanda. God, she's serious. I don't want kids and I certainly don't want to talk about it, definitely not here. Definitely not anywhere, if I have any say in it.'

'Why?'

'Think of the world those boys and girls back at the beach are inheriting. Why would anyone want to bring a baby into the climate change disasters, the totalitarian governments, the wars that already exist and the ones that will inevitably come.' He looked through the forest, shaking his head. 'Not sure we have a lot to talk about on that.'

Oh yes we do, Yolanda thought, but he's right, this is not the time for it.

Back at the campsite it had been taken for granted that Carey and Yolanda would join in for Christmas Eve dinner and be part of the combined Christmas lunch the next day. When they returned from the walk, they managed a surf without the kids. They showered and joined the group around the campfire, bringing across champagne, beer and nuts. The evening turned golden, then pink, taupe and finally gave way to the brilliance of a starry night sparkling down through the smoke and aroma of a barbecue. Yolanda leaned into Carey and whispered, 'The joy of family at Christmas.'

Christmas Day dawned under a pale, cloudless sky that went from pearl to pink to golden and finally arrived at cerulean. The intense blue stretched from the horizon, over the sandy shoreline, and spread dappled light over the campsite, flickering through the gum trees. Choruses of bird calls echoed around the forest, heralding the new day, announcing the birthday of a Messiah.

Near-naked bodies, adults and children, stood motionless in the clear waters of the ocean like devotees mesmerised by the great shining disc of the sun hovering above the horizon. Then the first wave rolled in and the figures dived under in a moment that looked almost choreographed, rinsing sleep out of their eyes and sluicing away their night dreams. Carey and Yolanda dived under the first wave with the other campers and surfaced laughing at the unexpected chill of the dawn sea.

After a day of indulgence, Christmas night slumbered under an indigo sky, encrusted with billions of stars, opened its eyes into Boxing Day then rolled through pleasure after pleasure into New Year. Carey and Yolanda were suspended in their own dreamlike state, seemingly without a care in the world.

'This is perfect,' Carey would sigh at moments of bliss, sunbaking on the sand, sucking the last strand of flesh from a lobster's claw or snuggling into Yolanda's neck, his hand wandering wantonly over her body, his erection straining at the thin terylene of his swimming briefs.

'Perfect,' Yolanda would murmur as she rolled on her side so that they were face-to-face and kissing.

'I want it to be always like this,' Carey murmured as the holiday drew to a close.

Neither of them wanted to give up the campsite, the beach, the bush and the freedom that had pervaded the two weeks after New Year. Over the second week of January, the other campers were one by one packing up their cars and moving out so that by the time Carey's booking came to an end there were none of the families they had spent time with. It was mid-January and Yolanda had to be back at school in the last week while Carey still had to work out what he wanted to do.

While they were packing the car, Carey casually said, 'I think I want to work with guys who've had some training. I wouldn't mind devising a piece about identity theft. Wouldn't that be interesting?'

Yolanda laughed. 'This place is an identity thief. I almost lost any sense of being a teacher. The only thing that mattered was whether to swim, eat, go for a hike or…' and she giggled, looking around to see if anyone was within hearing, '…to fuck.'

'Paradise,' Carey laughed.

Back in Sydney, Yolanda settled down to preparing for her senior classes. Carey started contacting independent theatre companies, having coffee with CEOs, managers, administrators and other directors. He was somewhat alarmed at the full extent of undermining that the COVID pandemic had had on the performing arts companies.

By mid-February he had registered for casual teaching and had scored a couple of days at a school an hour's train ride away. 'This is hopeless,' he complained to Yolanda.

'You could go back to teaching full-time,' she suggested.

Carey shook his head. 'I can't give up that easily. I want to work in the performing arts. There has to be something out there for me. Maybe I should start my own company.'

'And watch it fail like those other small companies?' Yolanda asked. She was starting to be a bit worried about being the sole income earner. They were all right in a way, but she also knew that Carey would be happier if he had his own project, an income and wasn't eating into his savings. She wondered if he wasn't still in a semi-holiday mood and thought about how she might shake him out of it into the familiar reality of work and income.

On a hot evening late in February, Carey took a phone call. 'Hang on a minute.' Carey was trying to get his head around what the woman on the other end of the phone had asked. 'Have I got this right? You want to work with me to devise a performance on the sexual and reproductive rights of women with disability?'

'Yes.'

'Wow, that would be quite an undertaking!'

The woman on the other end agreed then added, 'And we want it to include dance.'

'Dance?'

'Yes. Will you do it?'

'Look, I think you've got the wrong number here. I'm Carey Dansby. I'm a director, not a choreographer. I do drama, not dance. Who did you want to contact?'

Carey listened to a long rambling story about how the woman on the phone had seen a show of his last year, how she and her friends were blown away by the play and the dance in it. 'That's what we want you to do with us.'

We! Us! 'Sorry, who are you again?'

'Christine Lowell. I'm the artistic director of a dance/drama group called Wheel Women. That's spelt w-h-e-e-l.'

Carey chuckled. 'Wheel, real: that's cute.'

'Yes, we think so,' Christine replied, 'but there is another reason for calling the group Wheel Women.'

'What's that?' Carey assumed she was an ABI, acquired brain injury victim, and that the group had all been involved in motor vehicle accidents. He began preparing to end the conversation. *This Christine Lowell probably has the best of intentions, but it has nothing to do with me and my projects. Why would a woman with disability want to have children anyway?*

'Actually, we're called Wheel Women because we're all in wheelchairs.'

'What? Carey couldn't contain his laughter, but, realising the inappropriateness of it, quickly stopped. 'You're kidding me. You want a play about…about what you said, and you want dance in it?'

'That's right.'

Carey took a deep breath. 'Christine, there are no such things as rights to reproduce. If a woman wants a baby, then she can have one unless, you know…you know…unless she isn't able to.'

'You don't understand what women with disability are up against. The world doesn't understand. Most people are against the very idea. That's what we want to explore in a performance.'

'Listen, Christine, firstly I don't do dance. At its best, what I do could be called movement. Secondly, I know nothing about sexual and reproductive rights for women with a disability. Thirdly, I'm not at ease with wheelchairs on stage at the best of times. Fourthly, I do self-devised theatre which takes a long time to prepare and rehearse with people with disability. The show you saw took two years of development then six months of rehearsals to get it ready for performance. Fifthly, where is the money coming from? Do you have a solid budget? Lastly, is there a support team to work backstage during workshops, rehearsals and performances?'

There was a long silence. Carey was determined not to break the stalemate, not to go on talking, to let the truth sink in and put an end to it.

He turned round in his chair as Yolanda came into the room. She was holding two glasses of white wine. He took one, clinked her glass in a toast and swallowed a big mouthful.

Carey took the phone from his ear, covered the mouthpiece with his hand and mouthed to Yolanda the words, 'I think she's offended.'

'I'm not surprised,' Yolanda said. 'You went in pretty hard.'

Carey rolled his eyes at her. He switched over to speakerphone, motioning to Yolanda to stay and listen. She perched on the arm of a lounge chair, curious.

'Christine? Are you still there?'

'Yes.'

'Look, Christine, I…I'm not being rude. I was just trying to point out that the concept…' He was about to say, was a crazy pipedream, but switched to '…it would be difficult to mount such a production.' He paused to let that sink in. 'Dancers are always coming up with great ideas for performance. They have amazingly creative minds, but too often the ideas collapse on the practicalities. You know what I mean?'

There was another silence, which was broken when Christine said, 'What we want is to dance.'

'So go off and dance,' he said. 'You don't need me. Just do it.'

'Because we're in wheelchairs doesn't mean we can't dance.' Christine's voice had taken on a tone just short of strident.

A light went on in Carey's brain. Of course, he deduced, they get out of the chairs and dance. I got fixated on wheelchairs, couldn't see the obvious. Still don't want to do it. Doesn't have any traction for me.

'What you need, Christine, is a choreographer. And you should work with a woman, not a man. A woman would understand the issues better.'

The silence on the other end of the phone seemed as if it was going on forever.

'You see that, don't you?'

'We're not trained dancers.' Her voice was resigned, tremulous and struggling to conceal a depth of defeat.

Carey knew that feeling. He had been in this exact same situation himself many times. Great ideas need great loads of money to get them moving, but this lady doesn't have a cent is my guess, just a desire to get out there and strut her stuff. Good luck to her. It sounds like a worthy project, but I have my own stuff to sort.

He heard Christine clear her throat and ask, 'Are you interested?'

'Look, I'm not the creative you want, Christine. There are plenty of good women directors out there.'

Yolanda raised a questioning eyebrow at him. 'Why not have a go?' she mouthed.

'Look Christine, I can't do it, I'm sorry.'

'You mean you won't do it.'

'Same thing,' Carey said rather tersely. 'There's no point in my beating around the bush. It sounds like an interesting project and I wish you well with it.'

'Why shouldn't women with a disability, even an inheritable condition, be entitled to have disabled children like themselves?'

He was shocked at what she was saying. 'Deliberately pass on an inheritable disease to a baby? Are you serious?'

Christine cut in. 'It's already happening with some groups of disabled people. Communities of blind people who only want blind children because the parents will know how to bring them up. Deaf people, people who can't talk! They want children like themselves. Everybody wants their children to be like them. The world is changing Carey, and we, Wheel Women, want to have a voice about choices. Just think about it. Will you do that? I'll ring you in a week or so. Okay? Bye, Carey.' The phone went dead.

She's mad. Stark raving bonkers. Just think about it, she said. What is there to think about? The arrogance of the woman, presuming there are rights to inflict disabilities on innocent little babies.

'Do people want their children to be like them? I guess that's right, but to inflict a disability!' He looked at Yolanda, disbelief clenching his jaw.

Something about the look on her face stopped him short. Oh my God, he thought. Babies! She's still thinking about us. He recalled the way she'd been with the little kids over the holiday. He hadn't been the only Pied Piper. The littlies had been like ducklings following her around, playing games with her, competing to sit next to her at mealtimes, riveting attention on her as she read stories before their bedtime.

Women! Babies! The biological imperative! Yolanda wants children. That's what all those references to family over Christmas were about. And Christine and her Wheel Women friends want to argue the human right for their community to reproduce despite the risks.

Carey and Yolanda discussed sexual and reproductive rights for some time. Carey kept wanting to include men with a disability, but Yolanda checked him.

'What Wheel Women want to drive is the discussion about a woman's right to take control of her own body without being dictated to by men – or doctors or parents.' Yolanda's face was flushed.

'Not if that right comes at the cost of transferring a disability to a baby.'

'Why not? It's more than a question of political correctness. You said it yourself. It's about human rights, the right of any woman to have children.'

Carey put his head in his hands. 'Sorry, sorry. I'm not trying to trivialise the matter. I know it's complex, but Christine was hectoring me into accepting her proposal. Not that it's a proposal actually, more an expression of some vague politically correct idea.'

As they discussed the phone call, an argument developed about the rights of women and escalated into a shouting match about unresolved issues in their own relationship.

Yolanda attacked Carey about his expectation that she would do the cleaning, do the shopping and do the cooking. 'You can't even unstack the dishwasher until the next lot of dirty plates has piled up. And what about the washing?'

Carey was hard-pressed defending himself while opposing the right of disabled women to have babies.

'Oh yes,' Yolanda exploded, 'Mr Nice Guy to the world, but can't lift a hand in his own house. Why are you so selfish, Carey?'

Carey stormed out of the lounge room, got into his running shorts and sneakers and set off down the hill towards the park with Yolanda's parting shot, 'You shouldn't exercise after booze!' ringing in his ears.

He'd run about five kilometres when his will suddenly deserted him. He sat on a park bench, Yolanda's criticisms echoing in his head and Christine's rights mission niggling at his conscience.

Selfish! Am I selfish? Carey thought over the last few weeks since they had returned to Sydney. I've been in a slump. It's true, I didn't do any of the house things, kept avoiding the chores. Okay, I don't pull my weight. I hate all that stuff. It's dead boring – I suppose it is for everybody. Housework takes so much time, time I would rather spend on developing concepts for shows, not that that's happening at the moment, either.

There was a yell from the other side of the park. A group of people were having a picnic and some of the kids had got up a scratch cricket match. Families, he thought, I'm surrounded by them. It all looks so nice, but it gives me the heebie-jeebies when I think about it. Imagine having to organise the picnic – food, getting the kids ready, packing the cricket bats and balls and whatever other games they have in the car, then driving through traffic to get here.

He scrutinised the picnic group. They are all young, older than Yolanda and me, but of an age with us. They decided to have a family. Did those guys decide or did they just follow what their women wanted? Yolanda is thinking of it, wants us to talk about it. Why? Does she really want to bring children into this world? If I say I won't have kids, what then? Would she leave me, take up with another guy? Or go it alone?

I love her. I don't want to lose her. I want to go on having the fun times together. I guess that is selfish, but kids bugger up relationships between partners. And then there's that bleak future for humanity.

He looked at the picnickers. They all seemed pretty relaxed. Doesn't seem to be any fear of extinction there, he thought. Men and women, partners, married couples, sitting close together, laughing, calling to their kids, applauding a good hit and snuggling up to each other in sympathetic commiseration after one of their kids got bowled out. Maybe that's it. Kids bring a different kind of intimacy to relationships. What my mother calls maturity. 'You're not going to be young forever, Carey.'

There was another jubilant yell from the picnickers. One kid had her arms in the air in a victory salute to herself and a boy was patting her on the shoulder. Yeah, there is a joy in kids, in family. I get that. So am I being selfish about having children, selfish like not doing the housework? Maybe I am. Maybe I ought to be more like Christine and accept the possibility of having kids despite the risks. Populate and perish or populate or perish!

How on earth would Christine be able to organise a picnic like that in a wheelchair? How would a blind mother or a mother with muscular dystrophy organise that? There'd have to be someone to do the work, a husband or partner. That's doable. Disabled people have partners.

His mind homed in on the question of disabled and abled love matches. How on earth does an able-bodied man fall in love with a woman in a wheelchair? I would assume it works the other way. The person with a disability falling for some able-bodied man or woman. Why do I find the reverse so hard to understand?

Are my attitudes stuffed? I've been working with people with disabilities for five years. I know their emotional and sexual needs. Actually, they're just like the rest of us when it comes to the crunch. He reflected on the conversation with Christine. Perhaps I don't understand as much as I think I do.

There was a shout from the cricket game. Look at those kids, well-fed, clothed, happy. Good parenting for sure. Perfect kids, perfect families, heading for extinction. Perfectly imperfect! Everyone must want the perfect baby…except Christine, the Wheel Women. It was an interesting idea of Christine's that the perfect baby would be one that has her imperfections.

A flock of corellas swept down and landed on the ground a little way in front of him. Amidst a constant cacophony of calls they dug at the grass with their beaks, finding seeds and roots to eat. One of the birds was moving strangely and as he looked, Carey noticed that one of its claws was mangled. Was it from an accident or was it born with a gammy foot? A disabled parrot! The other corellas have accepted it. It seems to fit in perfectly with the flock. But it's not in a wheelchair and that's a big difference. The image of the corella in a wheelchair amused him and he let it linger in his mind until it was forced out by a totally unexpected thought. What if I did create a show with Wheel Women? Where would I start?

What was it Christine said – why aren't disabled women entitled to have children who are like them? But where does that leave the rights of the child, eh?

If I do the show, there will need to be a child.

The was a loud burst of laughter and cheering from across the park where some of the adults had joined the kids in cricket. Alarmed by the sudden noise, the corellas rose in a pulsating cloud of pink and white brilliance and arced across the park, streaking the greens of the trees with the lines and spaces of a raucous symphony. Carey desperately wanted to hold on to the picture of people and parrots before it dissolved. But it had been one of those rare moments of illumination which faded as the corellas disappeared behind a stand of paperbarks and the picnickers settled down to eating, drinking and talking.

Carey stood up and stretched in preparation for setting off on the return run. People, birds, they find partners, they mate and have babies. They expect the kids to be like them. What a shock if a woman gave birth to a corella! Would she be able to love it, to rear it?

Polanski's movie Rosemary's Baby flashed into his consciousness. That's what the movie was about. Rosemary's maternal instincts brought her to love the devil baby. It's the instincts that determine the love and care, not how the baby looks.

He looked over to the picnickers. Do any of them have hidden conditions that the kids will inherit? Did it even occur to them to have their DNA checked out? The more I think about the issues involved, the more intrigued I'm becoming.

He set off across the park. When he reached home, he ran through the house to the backyard, where he could hear Yolanda watering the herbs. He took her in his arms and hugged her, water splashing over both of them.

'Get off me, you idiot,' she laughed.

'Sorry! I don't know why I said those things.'

Yolanda pushed him away. 'Get off. You've wet me and you're sweaty, and you stink. Go and have a shower before I give you one here.'

Carey held her by the shoulders, smiling. 'I'll probably do the show Christine rang about.'

Yolanda frowned, confused. 'But…'

'I need to do a lot of research to see what the issues are, what the debates say, but I think it has a lot of potential dramatically, and…well, it will be something to do.'

Five weeks later, Carey was standing outside a church hall in the suburbs with four women in wheelchairs. The first impression he had was that they were about as unprepossessing as you could get. And yet, here they were, wanting to tackle the issues around sexual and reproductive rights for their community.

'Hi, I'm Annie.' The woman was beaming and extending a shaky hand to him.

Carey shook hands with Annie as Christine introduced Sue and Marissa.

'Let's go in,' Christine said. 'The minister gave me the key.' She moved up to the door and opened it. 'We have to clear up after us and leave the hall as we find it,' she called over her shoulder and swept inside, followed by the others.

The hall was like many other church halls, vaulted, with a large floor space and a stage at one end.

Carey pulled up a chair and sat down. 'I'd like to start by us getting to know each other.'

'Just before we begin,' Annie interrupted, 'I can't see how we're going to get on the stage.'

'We won't be on the stage,' Carey replied. 'The performance will be at ground level. I'll find a theatre where the stage area is at ground level and the seats are raked backwards and upwards.'

'That makes perfect sense,' Christine interrupted before Annie could ask more questions. 'It gives us plenty of room to dance and removes the access problems.'

'Okay,' Carey said, 'tell me a little about yourselves. Can I start with you, Sue.'

'Sure.' Sue spoke through an electronic voice machine which required her to type in anything she wanted to say. Carey hadn't encountered this means of communicating before. It was weird and he had to concentrate to get his hearing adjusted to the sound of the voice.

'I'm a solicitor. I work for the Solicitor General New South Wales. Mainly research on constitutional matters. Some contract work, leases on government premises.'

God, Carey thought, we can't have that on stage. I don't mind the machine, but I can't ask an audience to wait while Sue types in her dialogue then presses the speak button.

'Sue, can your voice machine pre-record? I mean if you have dialogue, can it be pre-recorded and ready to go on stage?'

Sue nodded vigorously and said in her own incomprehensible voice what Carey could only presume was confirmation that her speech could be pre-recorded.

'Okay, he laughed. 'That's good to know.'

He thought better of asking the others to talk about themselves, just in case there were similar constraints on dialogue. He changed tack.

'Let me ask from the outset…' Carey paused, a sudden compunction making him wonder if this wasn't a step too early in the process. He decided to press on. 'Do you think disabled women are entitled to have babies even if they transfer a genetic condition to the embryo?'

Sue erupted in a flurry of incomprehensible speech and furious typing on her voice machine. They waited until she finally looked up and pressed the speak button.

'Absolutely! I wanted to have a child, but everyone kept telling me I couldn't do it, wouldn't be able to look after it, couldn't risk passing my condition onto an infant. Over the years, I debated the matter back and forth in my mind and when I finally decided I did want a child, it was too late. I was menopausal, early onset.'

Sue was glaring at them while the voice read the message. There was a fire in her eyes which Carey guessed was fuelled by bitterness, resentment, frustration and a host of other emotions. Though he could feel the heat of Sue's anger, he realised that he had struck gold with that speech.

He looked around the group. The other women were looking at him and he felt a sense of expectation as to how he would respond.

He nodded, then spoke quietly. 'I want you to think about this.' Carey said. 'That speech would make fantastic theatre.' He waited to see if they were appalled by the suggestion, but there were those same, quiet intense stares focused on him, waiting. 'Would you be prepared to have the speech included in the play?'

Sue's eyes widened. Then her head jerked slightly and something akin to a smile crossed her face. She nodded. Her agreement was quietly dignified, an acceptance that the kind of theatre Carey was considering creating would be partly based on their own personal experiences, their stories in their own voices. This time when she spoke, Carey had no trouble understanding her.

'Yes.'

Marissa signalled she'd like to speak and they again had to wait while she typed into a voice machine what she wanted to say. She pressed the start button. 'I was born with cerebral palsy.'

'That's a birth accident, not a transmissible condition,' Christine interjected.

Marissa turned on Christine, shushing her for interrupting. When she spoke in her own voice, Carey reckoned he could understand up to a quarter of the words. He made a mental note that her dialogue would also have to be pre-recorded.

Marissa had gone back to typing into her voice machine and again pressed the play button. 'I agree with Sue. The difference between me and the others is that cerebral palsy is the result of a birth injury, an accident. It is not inheritable. If I had had a baby, it wouldn't have CP.'

'Whereas my baby would almost definitely inherit the muscular dystrophy I have,' Christine said.

Carey's mind was in overdrive as dramatic possibilities emerged from the conversation. He was lost in thought until Annie spoke.

'Do you want to know about me?'

'Yes, of course. Sorry, my mind is running on over the possibilities.'

'My primary disabilities,' Annie said, 'are brittle bones, so I won't be throwing any of these girls around.' She let out a rippling laugh, bringing a smile to Carey's face. 'And I have cognitive deficits. Learning lines might be a bit of a problem for me, but I'll give anything a go.'

Carey looked from Annie to Marissa. 'What about having babies?'

Annie shrugged. 'Don't know.'

Marissa spoke, but her language was so mangled it took some time for her to get out her response. Eventually she managed to say, 'Too hard.'

They sat in silence pondering that response. Too hard to decide on an issue like that, Carey wondered. Too hard to manage a pregnancy? Too hard on an infant to give it an inheritable condition? Except her condition is not genetic.

'That's it!' Carey slapped his thigh in his excitement as the germ of a narrative formed in his mind. 'Marissa could play the woman who has a baby, a healthy child.'

There was a babble of talk as the Wheel Women threw in their ideas about that.

Marissa was typing as fast as she could and stopped the chatter with a raised hand. She pressed the speak button on her voice machine. 'I can have an able-bodied husband and a child. Not a baby. That would be too difficult for me on stage. Why not have a teenager who can dance?'

'Brilliant,' Carey breathed. 'That's it.'

Christine held up her hand. 'So part of the drama is that Sue has left it too late to have a baby. Is she resentful of Marissa?

'And what about Annie? And what about me?'

'Hey,' Carey laughed, breaking the tension in Christine's questions. 'Really good crisis points, Christine. That's great for drama.' He drew in a deep breath. 'This is only the first session. Look how far we have come in just over an hour. There's a lot more ideas, personal experiences and research to work into this play and we have the rest of the year to work on it. At this rate, we may have a show drafted by Christmas and start rehearsals in the New Year.

Marissa had been busy typing a message into her voice machine. She pressed the speak button as the others leaned in to catch what she wanted to say. 'I want my son to be perfect.'

'Or daughter,' Christine corrected her.

Marissa shook her head and said so clearly there was no mistaking it. 'Son.'

Christine laughed. 'A perfect son. You don't want much, do you, Marissa?'

'What if he isn't perfect?' Annie asked.' What if he has disabilities? Or some imperfections?'

'We can make him any way we want,' Christine butted in. 'It's a play Annie, a fiction. The issues are real, but what happens on stage is completely made up. We aren't going to have an imperfect boy, Marissa wants a perfect child so that's what we'll have.'

Annie chipped in. 'Nobody's perfect.'

Carey leapt to his feet. 'Brilliant! Brilliant! That can be the working title.' The women looked at him, waiting for him to spell it out. 'Don't you see? The play can be called *Perfectly Imperfect*.'

Christine clapped her hands together. 'I love that.'

'Okay,' Carey said, standing up and stretching. 'Enough talking for today. It's been really productive, so thank you, ladies. Now, let me see you dance.'

The workshops turned from weeks to months and into a second year. By Easter, they had the first act pretty well developed and the entrance dance movement roughed out. There was plenty of dialogue in it. For Marissa and Sue, Carey insisted on a mix of electronic and actual voices.

'No one will understand a word we say,' Sue protested.

'Probably,' Carey grinned, 'but at least the audiences will know that you do have natural voices. Let them sit in their seats trying to work out what the words are that you are saying, then let them wonder at the miracle of electronics which let you have your say, clearly and succinctly.'

The second act reached a plateau during winter. There were head colds, various injuries and a worrying downward trend in Annie's general health which meant she was missing too many workshops. On the plus side, the project was moving towards finding a male dancer and a boy as well as a choreographer to create more dance in the piece.

Christine would take Carey aside from time to time to vent her worries about Annie. 'She'll never learn the dialogue, she can't follow the dance routines.'

Sue and Marissa were nodding.

Then Christine asked Carey, 'Can you do it without Annie?'

Carey had been asking himself this exact same question. He had discussed the issues with Yolanda.

'You can't exclude Annie now, not after all this time,' Yolanda said. 'Think of the work she has put in. Cutting her out would be devastating. No, you have to work around the deficits.'

Carey hugged her. 'You're right. I'll think of something. I want this resolved by the next rehearsal.'

He went upstairs and got into his running gear. When he came down, he called to Yolanda. 'I'm going for a run. I need to clear my head.' He set off and when he arrived at the park, he went to his favourite spot and sat cross-legged on the grass. Annie's dialogue, he thought. Let me put the story line together and see where I can cut the number of words she has to speak.

The big problem is in act two. Annie has a crucial role in that act. Her story is that she was pregnant at the same time as Marissa's character, but buckled to pressure and had a termination. Who would have been her support at the termination?

He tried to think his way into being pregnant with a disability and going to a clinic for an abortion. I just can't get into that space, he admitted to himself, defeated by the impossibility of a man in that situation. She would have needed another woman to be there. But who would that person have been?

An idea began to form. What if Sue and Annie were close friends back then? What if Annie told Sue of her predicament and Sue offered to be the support? That's it. Annie doesn't want family involved. She's pissed off with them because of the pressure they put on her to end the pregnancy. Yes, that's it. Sue knows the story so when Annie breaks down on stage and can't complete what she is saying, Sue takes over and finishes the story.

Carey stood up and stretched. That makes good drama. We might have a simple, mournful and short solo dance for Annie while Sue does the dialogue. Or a duet with Charlie.

When he told the Wheel Women at the next rehearsal, Christine declared that it wouldn't work.

Carey shook his head at her. 'Yes, Chris, it'll work. This is the way to make it work.'

It took another year for Carey to secure a small grant. He auditioned boy dancers at performing arts high schools and found the perfect lad to play Charlie. Somewhere along the way, a teacher suggested a friend of hers to play the father. Carey liked the guy and he was a very experienced dancer who thought the *Perfectly Imperfect* project was brilliant. Then Carey put out the word to the arts community that he was looking for a choreographer to create dance pieces with four women in wheelchairs. Within a day or two, Surprise Movement Theatre got in touch and recommended a woman who had done some great work with them. When they met for the first time, the Wheel Women loved her and she agreed to do the show.

Then Carey sweet-talked a lighting and set designer into doing the work for a lower fee than the going rate. They were part of a theatre company which had begun years before as an actor's collective and had great empathy for community arts, despite now being a professional operation. The final success was when Carey managed to secure a two-hundred-seat studio space in a large theatre complex. With all this in place, he began a mammoth promotional campaign, finished the storyboard and tech specs and ramped up the number of rehearsals to two a week.

When *Perfectly Imperfect* opened, it ran for seven performances and played to almost full houses. The show got standing ovations at four of those and an unexpected – and good – review in a leading daily newspaper.

'Well, so much for not doing disability theatre projects,' Yolanda joked as he drank a glass of white wine a couple of days after closing night.

He leant over and kissed her. 'Won't you join me in a celebratory drink?'

She held his head in her hands and looked him in the eyes. 'I'll have a celebratory drink with you in about eight or nine months' time.'

'Nine months?' Carey pulled away abruptly, staring at her, a puzzled frown on his face. 'You're not…I mean…are you…?'

Yolanda nodded.

Carey leapt to his feet. 'You decided the question for me, for both of us! You had no right.'

'Right!' Yolanda adopted the high moral ground. 'You've just spent three years working on *Perfectly Imperfect*. That show was about rights, Carey, the drama of women who are talked out of getting pregnant, who decide too late they do want to conceive and are caught out by menopause or some other condition. We talked about women having babies. We even talked about us having babies.'

'That was theatre, not actually having babies,' he snapped.

'Actually having babies is what we talked about.' She paused to regain her composure. 'Actual, living little babies.' She held his gaze, defiant. This was crunch time for both of them. Carey had to make a decision and stop palming her off about babies. Either he's in or…

Carey was angry. How could she do this? It's entrapment. She's tricked me. He stormed out of the lounge room, turned on his heel and stormed back in. 'Trust! You've destroyed my trust in you.' Carey was breathing heavily. He couldn't look at her. 'You never said you wanted to start the family thing now.'

Yolanda bridled. 'Three years, Carey, three years. I tried, Carey, tried so many times over that time, but you couldn't, wouldn't, didn't want to discuss it. You ignored me. Talking to you about having a baby was like talking to a brick wall. You always had something else to do – workshops, scriptwriting, rehearsals, auditioning dancers, negotiating a venue, promotion, writing grant applications. Or you were too tired to discuss it. And if it wasn't any of those things, it was running or swimming or some other fitness thing. Plenty of sex, but never any time to explore the possible implications of lovemaking further.'

They glared at each other. 'You know I want children. Even in this shitty world, I want to bring up a family.'

'No!' he exclaimed. 'I always made time for you. I listened to the problems you were having at school, discussed your decisions. We went out – movies, cafés, went to dinners at your colleagues' houses, had holidays. I have always been here for you.'

'Except for this one, big, life-changing decision. You pushed me away every time I brought it up.'

They stared at each other, both uncertain of how to get out of this deadlock.

Yolanda was flushed. Trust, she thought. He's right. I should have told him I was going off the pill. I should have warned him.

Carey felt a chill down his spine. While one part of him wanted to refute what she was saying about him, another part had to admit it was true. She had brought up the subject so many times and he had never taken her seriously. Was I hoping she would get sick of asking and drop it? As if!

Do I want to become a father or not? He put his fingers to his temple to hide the pulse that was beating into a frenzy the words baby, father. He slumped cross-legged onto the floor, breathing heavily, bringing his pulse under control before he spoke. 'Okay, I have been avoiding the question of babies. It's not that I don't like babies, not that the idea of kids of my own isn't appealing. It's about this world, Yolanda. You said it yourself, this shitty world.'

She spoke quietly, her tone measured. 'I'm prepared to risk bringing a family into this world because I think that eventually those pig-headed leaders will be forced to act on cleaning up the mess. The future will be different, but I think the next generation will collaborate with others to develop the wherewithal to create liveable environments. Our children will be part of that.' She paused, gauging his reaction. 'We have to have hope, otherwise what's the point?'

'Wow!' Carey was taken aback. 'You've never said that before.'

'We've never thrashed this out face-to-face before. I needed to think through my position clearly because I knew you would be angry if I became pregnant without your knowledge.'

'But you went ahead anyway. How far gone are you?'

'I'm not gone. Still here, Carey. I'm bringing new life into the world – our child.'

They sat for a long while in silence, engrossed in their thoughts, not looking at each other, stealing secretive glances when each thought the other wasn't looking.

Our child! He glanced at Yolanda. She looked exactly the same as she always did. Our baby! It sounded thrilling and terrifying to Carey. It had happened without his knowing and this made it weirdly unreal for him. One orgasm and I didn't even know how much more it meant than the pleasure. I don't even know which time it happened.

Confusing emotions rampaged through him. Then out of the tumult of anger, excitement, amazement, concern, a completely unexpected emotion emerged which threw him off guard. He wanted to go and put his hand on her belly, but felt constrained by the argument they'd been having. She looked up and held his gaze.

I love her. I don't want to live without her. I don't want to be like those men who desert their girlfriends when they find out they're pregnant he thought. God, Carey, a woman's right to choose even at the risk of losing her man. He blinked. She was still staring at him, impassive, but he knew that she was also waiting for whatever was to come from him.

'A woman's right to choose,' he murmured.

Yolanda's face relaxed, but she didn't say anything.

'You've tricked me and that was wrong,' he muttered.

'I know,' she admitted.

'You're going to have it no matter what I do.'

Yolanda didn't move for some seconds, then slowly nodded.

Carey stood up. 'We've got a lot of repairing to do, Yolanda,' he murmured. Yet the desire to touch her urged him forward. 'Can I put my hand on your belly?'

She laughed and held her arms out to him, nodding. 'Come here, Dad.'

Nonny

After school one day, Rikki Selwood came up beside Nonny on the way to the bus stop. He swung his bag into Nonny's legs, making him stumble.

Nonny straightened himself. He was staring into Rikki Selwood's eyes. A storm was raging in those eyes. Dark clouds rolled across them from under the eyelids. Lightning flashed across the clouds. Rain poured down in gushing torrents. A howling wind tore around the eyes. Rikki Selwood's eye-weather made him look wild, unpredictable and deranged.

'What are you staring at, freak?' Rikki Selwood sneered. He shoved Nonny very hard, making him fall to the ground.

Nonny's face was close to the pavement. He could see little cracks in the surface. Do I have little cracks in my surface? he wondered. The pavement had an unpleasant smell and was covered in grime, just like Rikki Selwood.

Nonny's school backpack was close to his hand. However, the recorder case had been flung out of the backpack when it hit the ground. It was lying on the pavement where any passer-by might tread on it and break it.

I have to get my recorder off the ground before someone stands on it, Nonny thought.

Nonny picked himself up. Rikki Selwood stood looking at him, a nasty grin on his face. Nonny saw his knees were grazed and splotched with blood. Cracks! He was determined not to cry. But the first tears were already beginning to sting his eyes.

Rikki Selwood laughed. It was a harsh, humourless laugh. Then Rikki Selwood started chanting, 'Cry baby, cry baby.'

Nonny was scared that Rikki Selwood would hit him again. Nonny looked down to avoid Rikki Selwood's eyes and to check that his recorder was safe. He was too scared to reach for it in case Rikki Selwood did something to damage it.

Nonny wished his big sister Fleur was here to protect him. She'd know what to do.

Fleur was having a cello lesson in the big house further along the street. Nonny could hear the cello through the open window. He was to meet Fleur at the house when the lesson finished.

Nonny momentarily blanked out where he was as he listened. The music was beautiful. Fleur was preparing for her Fifth Grade cello exam. Nonny would have to wait until the lesson finished. Then they would catch the bus home. At home, there would be no more Rikki Selwood. His bag would be in his bedroom and his recorder case on his workstation.

Nonny bent over to pick up his recorder case from the ground, but there was a foot standing on it. Rikki Selwood's foot. Please don't break it, Nonny prayed silently, wishing he was twelve years old and bigger than Rikki Selwood. But Nonny was only nine years old and small for his age.

Most people liked Nonny very much, but there were exceptions. Exceptions like you know who. And that puzzled Nonny. Why is Rikki Selwood mean to me?

A voice shouted. 'Oi, you!'

A dog barked. 'Woof, woof!

The noises came from Mrs Pettibel's front gate. Mrs Pettibel owned one of the Safe Houses on the way from the school to the bus stop. She was coming out of her garden with Blip, her dog.

Rikki Selwood took off down the street, running as fast as his legs could carry him. He disappeared around the corner, heading towards the bus stop.

Mrs Pettibel came out of her garden and helped Nonny pick up his things. Not that he needed help. He checked his recorder case as Mrs Pettibel handed him his bag. The recorder wasn't damaged.

'You shouldn't let him bully you,' Mrs Pettibel said to Nonny.

Blip was prancing around, barking loudly until Mrs Pettibel told her to be quiet. She was a big, black labradoodle. Blip obeyed instantly and nuzzled Mrs Pettibel's hand with her wet nose.

Nonny put the recorder in his bag.

'Come inside and let me clean the blood off that scratch,' Mrs Pettibel said.

Nonny knew this was the right thing to do. But he didn't want to miss Fleur when she came out after her lesson. He couldn't decide what to do, so he just stood there staring at Mrs Pettibel with his big, brown eyes.

Blip sniffed at the blood on Nonny's knee.

'No, Blip.' Mrs Pettibel grabbed the dog collar and pulled Blip back to her side. 'Wait by the gate, Nonny. I'll get something to clean the blood off. Stay with Nonny, Blip.'

The dog sat by the gate, watching Nonny.

Mrs Pettibel had just finished cleaning the wound and putting a Band-Aid on it when Fleur called down the street. She was standing outside the big house with her cello case in one hand and a frown on her face. She hurried towards them. Blip ran up to her barking madly and sniffing the cello case.

Now that Fleur had finished her lesson, Nonny wanted to go home. He kept tugging at his sister's sleeve, but Fleur and Mrs Pettibel were talking. They were talking about him.

Blip started barking at a dog that had appeared at the other end of the street. Nonny wanted to go home more than ever because Blip was being noisy and the barking hurt his ears. He tugged at Fleur's sleeve.

'Did you say thank you, Nonny?'

Nonny shook Mrs Pettibel's hand by way of thanking her. Then he and Fleur set off to the bus stop.

'We've missed the bus,' Fleur said as she looked at the timetable on a pole. 'The next one isn't for another fifteen minutes.' She was annoyed. 'Come on. Let's sit. We have to wait.'

Nonny sat quietly. He was upset about Rikki Selwood and he knew Fleur blamed him for missing the bus. That's two bad things that happened after school, he thought. He touched Fleur on the arm to let her know he was sorry. Then he touched her arm a second time and looked up into her eyes to see if she understood and accepted the apology.

'That's all right,' Fleur said. 'It's not your fault.'

But Nonny thought that Fleur did blame him for missing the bus.

Nonny tugged at Fleur's sleeve again. When she looked at him, he indicated that he wanted to go to the toilet.

Fleur yelled at Nonny. 'Why didn't you say so when we were at Mrs Pettibel's? Or when we walked past my cello teacher's house?'

Nonny indicated that he had to go. It was urgent.

'There's no toilet here,' Fleur said sharply. 'You just have to wait until we get home.'

Nonny knew he couldn't wait. He pointed to the park behind them where there was a public toilet. He had to go. Nonny stood up and put on his backpack.

'Leave your bag,' Fleur said. 'Just go. Hurry, Nonny.'

Nonny didn't want to leave his bag. The recorder was in it. That was his responsibility. He needed to be sure it wouldn't fall out again.

Nonny walked as fast as he could and went into the toilet. He was doing a big wee when a man walked in and stood beside him.

'Hello,' the man said.

Nonny didn't answer.

'What's your name?' the man asked.

Nonny was very scared. He couldn't finish his wee.

'Do you want to touch my dickie?' the man asked.

Nonny didn't want to touch the man. He didn't want to be in the toilet with the man. What the man had said was horrible.

Nonny was afraid. He wanted to be with Fleur. She would know what to do.

Nonny pulled up his shorts, grabbed his backpack and ran out of the toilet. He was so scared he didn't even wash his hands.

When he got back to the bus stop, he sat close to Fleur. He was trembling.

'What's wrong?' Fleur asked. Nonny could hear in her voice that she was still cross about missing the bus. He didn't tell her about the man.

Then Nonny had another thought. It was a scary thought. What if the man came and sat next to him at the bus stop?

Nonny felt the tears coming again, but before they got further than the front of his eyes, the bus came. Nonny and Fleur got on the bus. The man was nowhere to be seen. Even so, Nonny felt sick all the way home.

When he walked into his house and saw his mother, Nonny burst into tears.

'Darling,' his mother said, coming to him. 'What's wrong, Nonny?'

Nonny's mother held him in her arms as he cried. Fleur told her about Rikki Selwood and how talking to Mrs Pettibel had made them late for the bus.

'I'll talk to Mrs Pettibel tomorrow,' mother said. She wiped Nonny's eyes. 'I'll ask her what happened. She won't mind keeping an eye out for you. Then I'll come to school and talk to your teacher about Rikki.'

Nonny didn't want that. It would only lead to more trouble with Rikki Selwood. He shook his head at his mother. She must not complain to the teachers.

Mother looked at Nonny. 'Did anything else happen?' she asked.

Nonny wouldn't look at his mother. He stared at the floor as mother asked Fleur if anything else had happened.

Fleur didn't know about the man in the toilet. Nonny hadn't told her at the bus stop. She was annoyed with him for making them miss the bus. He didn't want to get in any more trouble.

During supper, Nonny couldn't stop thinking of the man in the toilet. Later, when he was tucked up in bed, mother turned off the bedroom light and kissed Nonny goodnight. But he could see the man. He was standing close to his bed, asking him his name, asking if he wanted to touch his dickie. The picture happened over and over again. It was horrible. Nonny cried himself to sleep and the man in the toilet went there with him.

The next morning, Nonny felt sick and didn't want to go to school.

His mother felt his forehead. 'You don't have a temperature,' she said. 'Have some breakfast and see how you feel then.' Mother looked at him. He was pale and had dark rings around his eyes. He looked on the verge of tears so she said, 'I'll ask Fleur to walk you to the school gate so you needn't be afraid of Rikki Selwood.'

Nonny shook his head until his mother held it in her hands to stop him. 'Hey, Nonny, you love school and this is the day one of the parents comes in and tells the class about their work.'

Nonny had forgotten what day it was. He really liked hearing what the parents did while the children were at school. He liked the sense of a world continuing outside the school gate, a world of people working in offices, from home, of people shopping and going to a café to meet friends. It made everything in its right place and he liked that because it meant that school was the right place for him, for all children – except for Rikki Selwood. Nonny couldn't think of a place where Rikki Selwood should be, but he thought it shouldn't be here in his primary school.

After his mother had got him upstairs and into the shower, Nonny was feeling a little bit better. When he came downstairs in his uniform, Fleur was waiting impatiently at the front door, her schoolbag on her back. Because Nonny had taken so long getting ready, Fleur set off at a cracking pace so mother only had time to give him a glancing goodbye kiss on the cheek. Fleur deposited Nonny at the school gate then raced back to the bus stop for her school bus.

The bell rang and the children lined up in their class groups. Nonny's place in the line was behind Paul and in front of Anastasia. The three of them sat together around a table in the classroom and Gemma made the fourth in the group. Gemma had something called Down syndrome. She was nice, but would sometimes annoy the others and do silly things.

Nonny went to the library at recess and made a plan for lunchtime. So, when he'd finished his lunch, he sneaked back into the classroom. It was against the rules, but he had to get his recorder. That was part of the plan to avoid Rikki Selwood.

Clutching the recorder in his hand, he crept down the hall and climbed the stairs to the music room. It felt strange being inside when there were no children and no teachers. He put his hand on the knob and turned it, but the music room door didn't open. That was very confusing. It hadn't occurred to Nonny that a classroom would be locked. They don't want children in there without a teacher, he reasoned.

He walked along the upstairs hallway and found the door to the next classroom open. He went in and closed the door behind him. Perching himself on a work desk, he got out his recorder and prepared to play. Nonny nearly fell off the table when the door burst open.

Rikki Selwood barged into the room, eyes all rolling storm clouds and lightning flashes. 'You're in trouble, freak!' Rikki Selwood roared. 'You're not allowed in here at lunchtime. Give me that.' He reached across and snatched the recorder out of Nonny's hands. 'You look stupid with this and you sound awful,' Rikki Selwood jeered. 'I'm going to break it so I don't ever have to listen to you playing it again.'

Nonny jumped off the table, bent on saving his precious recorder. He landed on Rikki Selwood, sending them both flying to the floor. The recorder shot across the room as Rikki Selwood let out a cry of pain.

'Get off me, you freak! I'll kill you!' Rikki Selwood was thrusting and twisting on the floor, trying to get Nonny off him.

'Stop! What do you think you are doing? Get off the floor immediately.' Mrs Fidge stood towering in the doorway, her hands on her hips and a terrible frown on her face.

Nonny got up and Rikki Selwood stood beside him. Both the boys were scared of Mrs Fidge. She was the school principal. Mrs Fidge could expel a child if she wanted to and Nonny was sure that's exactly what she was about to do to them.

Mrs Fidge bent down and picked up the recorder. She examined it then placed it on one of the tables. 'Sit!' she commanded, pointing to two chairs.

The boys sat down.

'I saw him come inside, miss. I thought he was up to no good.' Rikki pointed at Nonny.

Rikki Selwood was trying to sound innocent and Nonny was frightened that Mrs Fidge would believe him.

'No, Rikki.' She sat on the table and picked up the recorder. 'That's not it at all, is it?'

'Yes, miss, honest, miss, I saw him creep in here. He's always creeping around. He's a creep.' Rikki Selwood sniggered.

Mrs Fidge put a finger to her lips and gently shushed at him. When she took her finger away, Nonny thought she had a kinder look on her face.

'You see, boys, we have a problem here, a bullying problem. We have a no bullying rule at this school. I think that rule has been broken.' She paused and looked at Rikki Selwood. 'Has it been broken, Rikki?' she asked quietly.

Rikki Selwood didn't answer.

Nonny stared at Rikki Selwood, then turned back to look at Mrs Fidge. Am I the problem? he wondered.

'Hmmm,' Mrs Fidge sighed. 'What are we going to do about this… this bullying thing?'

Neither boy spoke. Nonny knew what he wanted. He wanted Rikki Selwood to be expelled. As soon as he thought of that word, Nonny realised how bad that would be, even for Rikki Selwood. All he wanted was for Rikki Selwood to leave him alone in the playground. And for him, Nonny, to be able to sit at the table with Paul, Anastasia and Gemma and to play in the recorder band.

Mrs Fidge broke the silence. 'What we need is an agreement. The agreement is that you two boys keep out of each other's way. Do you think you can do that, Rikki?'

'Yes, miss, but what about him?'

Mrs Fidge stared at Rikki Selwood for so long that Nonny began to feel scared as to what she was going to do. He wanted to leave, wanted for this afternoon to be over.

Then Mrs Fidge took a deep breath and seemed to grow taller as she stood up. 'Okay, one more thing,' Mrs Fidge said. Her voice had become very serious. 'Rikki, I am going to have to call your parents in again.'

'No, miss! Please, miss! Don't tell my dad. Please, miss.'

Nonny was shocked to see Rikki Selwood trembling and his face turning red.

'Please, miss, don't call my parents. I'll be good. I promise, miss.'

The long silence that followed Rikki Selwood's outburst was interrupted by the end-of-lunchtime bell. Mrs Fidge swept her eyes over the boys. Nonny thought that he and Rikki Selwood seemed to shrink under the glare of her look.

'Go to class now, boys,' she said. 'When the morning bell goes tomorrow, come to my office and we can talk about how you can keep out of each other's way. I'll let your teachers know where you are.'

Am I going to be in trouble tomorrow? Nonny wondered.

Mrs Fidge was thoughtful after the two little boys left. What to do about Nonny? He's locked himself away in a silent world of his own, never uttering a sound. And Rikki – his reaction when I talked about calling in his parents again was alarming. Something wrong there?

Mrs Fidge went down to her office and phoned Nonny's mother at work to discuss the situation.

Back in the classroom, Nonny felt better. All the children were a bit frightened of Mrs Fidge, but she's nice, he decided. Then a dark thought struck him. Is tomorrow when she is going to be angry with us for being inside at lunchtime?

When the bell rang to end lessons for the day, Nonny carefully packed his bag and hurried off to Mrs Pettibel's Safe House, where he would wait for Fleur to pick him up. He kept a look out for Rikki

Selwood, but his tormentor didn't come by. That made Nonny feel better. He went into the back garden and played throwing a ball with Blip. Nonny liked the way Blip always fetched the ball and brought it back, dropping it at his feet.

Fleur and Nonny thanked Mrs Pettibel for looking after Nonny and set off for the bus stop. Nonny was determined not to look at the park. However, his head had a different idea. It kept turning so that he had to sneak a look at the toilet. Nobody there. Nonny felt relieved, but his head kept turning to the park to make sure.

Nonny ran into his house ahead of Fleur and was immediately wrapped up in his mother's arms. Fleur hesitated in the hall. Her mother smiled and blew her a kiss. Fleur went into her bedroom and began practising the cello.

During dinner, Nonny's mother told him Mrs Fidge had rung her at work and told her about the confrontation with Rikki Selwood.

'Do you want me to come to the meeting tomorrow morning?' his mother asked.

Nonny shook his head vigorously. He definitely did not want his mother to be there. He didn't want to be there either, but had to be. He certainly didn't want to be there with Rikki Selwood, but knew that was going to happen.

That night, his mother tucked him up in bed, kissed his cheek and stroked his hair the way she knew he liked it. 'If there is anything worrying you, Nonny, you know it helps to tell someone. Talking about it is one way of stopping the worry.'

Nonny looked at her with his big eyes. He couldn't tell her about the man in the toilet and his thing. It had been horrible and he loved his mother too much to upset her. It was bad enough that Mrs Fidge had rung her at work and told her about Rikki Selwood. The toilet thing would have to remain his secret.

As his mother turned off the light and pulled his door to, Nonny knew that the man in the toilet was standing at the foot of his bed and was smiling at him. He would always be there now, forever and ever.

Caught in the Middle

'And Matt Jones takes a fantastic intercept from Josh Tran. He rolls in for the winning points! Can he slam dunk on his blades? He lines up – and he scores! What a shot! Jones is on a high. The crowd goes wild. Next stop Olympic gold!'

Josh always called a running commentary as they played their version of extreme basketball after school at the skate park. Rollerblades, skateboards and jump ramps at each goal were all part of the game.

'Who's the man, Tran! Who's the man?' Matt pulled his signature yellow T-shirt over his head and turned a perfect circle on his blades. Josh gave him a high five and they did a victory lap together.

The thing about Matthew Jones was that he was nice to people and never mean. That's how Josh came to join the group one day when he cracked Matt up with one of his silly jokes. At first he hadn't been any good at basketball, but he loved the game and the others accepted him because he made them laugh.

Matt had taught Josh to dribble and pass and on weekends they spent hours shooting goals. So it was no surprise that Matt had just been voted captain of the under-13s team and Josh the vice-captain.

It had been a good day. After the game, Matt bladed the three blocks home.

As he approached the house, his dog, Buster, started barking and hurling himself against the garden gate.

'What are you doing outside?'

The dog put his paws on Matt's shoulders and licked his face.

'Okay, get down,' Matt laughed.

Matt pushed the front door, but it was locked. He peered through the lounge room window and called, 'Mum! Sally! Mum!'

Puzzled, he looked around. The red station wagon was not in the drive. For a moment, he wondered if he was supposed to meet them somewhere. No, that wasn't it. He reached for the hidden key above the window and opened the door.

Dropping his bag in the hall outside his room, he patted Buster saying, 'Mum's not here. Come on, let's go and watch cartoons.'

It was only when he turned off the TV that he realised it was getting dark. 'Six o'clock! Where is everybody?' He decided to try Mum on her mobile phone, but there was no answer.

An uneasy feeling came over him. He went to the window and looked out. 'Something's wrong, Buster. Maybe I'll ring Dad.'

'Dad? It's me, Matt.'

'Hi, mate! What's doing?' His father's voice on the other end of the phone was reassuring.

'Where are Mum and Sally? They're not here. And Mum's not answering her mobile.'

There was silence at his father's end.

Matt suddenly felt frightened. 'Dad! What's wrong? Where are they? It's nearly dark and they're not home. You don't think they've had an accident, do you?'

'No, I'm sure they're all right. Just hang on. I'll finish up here. Be home in twenty minutes. Okay?'

Matt dashed about the house turning on all the lights. Buster thought it was a great game. As his father's car pulled into the driveway, Matt and Buster ran out.

'Dad! Dad, have you heard from them?'

'No, I don't know what's going on.'

Matt followed his father into the house. When they reached the main bedroom, Mr Jones stood in front of the open wardrobe clenching his fists tightly. It was empty. Matt could see his father was trying to stop his hands from shaking. He'd never seen him like this and it was scary. His father marched past him up the hallway, into Sally's bedroom and opened the wardrobe. Empty!

By the time Matt appeared in the doorway, Mr Jones's face had gone pale. Neither of them said a word. They just stood there staring into Sal's empty wardrobe. Then slowly an awful thought came into Matt's mind. The longer the silence went on, the bigger and bigger the idea grew until he couldn't bear it any more.

'Dad? Has Mum left?'

His parents had been arguing a lot lately, especially at night when he and Sally had gone to bed. One night there had been yelling and a crashing sound. In the morning, he saw his father's broken coffee mug in the rubbish bin.

Matt sat on the bed and put his arms around Buster. 'Has she, Dad?' Suddenly he was feeling very shaky.

'I think I know where they are.' This time his father's voice did not reassure him.

Matt followed his father into the lounge room. Mr Jones picked up the landline phone and dialled.

'That's Aunt Janet's number.'

His father nodded.

'Janet, hi, it's Gordon. Is Penny there? I need to speak to her.'

The landline was on speakerphone. 'Yes, she's here, but she doesn't want to speak to you, Gordon.'

'Just put her on, Janet.'

There was a pause. 'She wants to talk to Matt,' said Janet.

'Your mum wants a word.' He handed over the phone.

'Mum? What's happening?'

Mr Jones grabbed the phone. 'Penny! What in the name…' The line went dead. Mr Jones slammed the phone down and looked at Matt. 'She hung up,' he said angrily. 'Your mother hung up on us.'

Matt fought back tears. Buster nuzzled his wet nose into Matt's hand.

'Into the car,' Mr Jones ordered as he snatched up his keys. 'We're going over there.'

'Come on, Buster.'

'No, leave him.'

The look on his father's face warned Matt not to argue. They drove to his aunt's house in silence, but Matt felt funny in his tummy.

'Wait here.'

Matt did as he was told. His father got out of the car. There was no sign of Sally or his mother, or her car.

Matt heard his father knock and watched as Aunt Janet opened the door. Matt could see that she didn't want to let his father in. She kept shaking her head as he argued with her, gesturing towards Matt in the car. Matt couldn't make out the words but he could hear the anger in his father's voice.

When Aunt Janet tried to close the door, Matt was shocked to see his father push past her. He slunk down in the seat hoping she wouldn't notice him. Tears were stinging his eyes.

When Mr Jones came back out of the house, he marched towards the garage and yanked the heavy door open. There was no sign of the red station wagon. Where were Mum and Sally? They had been here only about ten minutes ago.

Matt's misery grew as his father stormed back into the car and slammed the door.

'I don't believe this,' he said, and drove off.

Neither of them spoke on the way home. Matt was struggling to suppress sobs that kept welling up in him. The car swung into their driveway and his father turned off the engine. His hands were still gripping the steering wheel. They just sat there. Matt could hear Buster barking at the front door, but didn't dare get out of the car. Then he couldn't stand the sound of Buster's yelping and scraping at the door.

'Dad! Dad, are we going inside?'

His father seemed not to hear. Then suddenly, without saying a word, he opened the car door and strode to the veranda. Matt didn't know what to do. Mum and Dad have never had a fight like this before, he told himself. Why won't she even talk to him now?

Suddenly his father appeared at the car window as if nothing had happened. 'Come on, son. Let's get something to eat. You hungry?' He was smiling, but Matt could see that he was acting. 'How about a nice steak with potatoes and broccoli?'

Matt hated broccoli. 'That'd be great, Dad.' He had managed to control his shaking and steady his voice. He got out of the car and Buster leapt all over him. When he walked into the kitchen, his father was standing with his hands pressed against the wall. His eyes were closed.

'Dad?' Matt whispered.

His father didn't move. Matt started shaking again.

There were so many questions that he wanted to ask, but it was as if his dad had forgotten that he was there. He turned and went to his bedroom, shutting the door quietly behind him. He could feel tears stinging just under his eyelids. Buster whimpered and put his head in Matt's lap.

It was then that he saw his mother's note on his pillow.

My darling Matt

Please don't be upset. I know this is all very sudden, but I need a bit of a break. You know Dad and I haven't been getting along lately. Sal and I are going to Uncle Rod's farm for a short time. I'll tell the school that Sal is away with me.

Term ends this Friday and I'd like you to come up on the Saturday morning train for the holidays. It's only a two-hour trip. I'll ask your father to drive you to the station and pick up the ticket. I've packed a bag for you and it's in your cupboard. Don't forget your windcheater. It gets really cold up there.

Dinner's in the microwave. Heat it for five minutes. Take it out and stir it around with a spoon, then give it another two minutes. There's enough for you and your father. Ice-cream is in the freezer. Don't forget to feed Buster.

Love you a lot

See you soon

Mum

PS I'll call you tonight when we arrive at Uncle Rod's.

Matt jumped when the phone rang. He'd been sitting beside it waiting, but still it startled him. After showing his father the note, they'd agreed that Matt should answer the call.

'Mum? When are you coming home?' Matt's mouth felt dry.

'Didn't you get my note, darling? I left it on your pillow.'

'Why couldn't I come with you and Sal? Why did you leave me behind, Mum?'

'I haven't left you, darling. I explained everything in the note. I just need a bit of thinking space.'

'About what? You can think here, can't you?' He could hear the whine in his voice, but he didn't care.

'No I can't.' His mother's voice was definite. 'And what with rehearsals for the school play, band practice and the game on Thursday evening, I couldn't drag you away this week. Year Six is your priority right now.'

'I don't care about any of that. I want to be with you! You don't love me!' Matt shouted.

His father took the phone. 'Are you happy now, Penny? Penny?' He looked at Matt. 'She's hung up again.'

Matt snatched the phone. 'Mum! Mum!' The phone was dead. He was about to throw it across the room when his father grabbed his arm. They glared at each other.

'Matthew, that's enough. It's late. Go to bed.'

Matt stomped up the hall without saying goodnight. Saturday couldn't come soon enough.

The days to the weekend seemed to slow down, creeping through classes in which he was hardly concentrating, dawdling in and out of handball at recess and lunchtime, and over the boring evening meal.

Finally, Friday afternoon arrived and he was driving with his father to the station.

'I'll pick you up in two weeks, on Sunday midday. The train gets in at five past twelve.' his father said. 'Tell Sally I love her. I miss her.' His father gave him an awkward hug and he boarded the train.

His mother and Sally were at the station when the train pulled in. Matt had been so looking forward to this weekend, to seeing his mum and Sally, but now that he was here he felt out of place – out of place at home with his dad and out of place here in the country.

On the drive to his uncle's, Sally fired questions at him, but Matt felt so tongue-tied he could only muster up monosyllabic answers. That night his dreams were full of him in little toy trains which kept going off the rails and disappearing into the sky, around a hill or simply fading out of the dream altogether.

'Come on, boys! Rise and shine! There's work to be done.'

Although the last week of term had seemed to drag, on the farm the days raced by. Uncle Rod woke them all early each morning. After breakfast, he would allocate tasks to be done before the day's adventures could begin.

'Rory, you're in the dairy to help me with the milking. Will, you feed the horses. Matt, you can collect the eggs with Sally then come up to the dairy.'

'Matt, I'll show you how I collect the eggs all by myself,' Sally piped up excitedly as she trailed behind him.

The older sister, Lauren, stayed behind to stack the dishwasher and wash the breakfast things. Before the cousins prepared to set out to do their chores, she suggested a plan for the rest of the day. 'Why don't we all meet back here in an hour and then go down to the swimming hole? Is that all right, Dad?'

Uncle Rod nodded and Lauren whooped. 'Later, we can go and see the balancing rocks at the top of the hill and be back for lunch.'

'Hey, Dad, will you give us rides on the tractor today?' chipped in Rory.

And that is how the days passed, full of fun on the farm, fresh milkshakes with milk from the vats in the dairy, swimming every day and rides on the horses and tractor with Uncle Rod. Matt wished this holiday could go on forever. The days he liked best were when it was his turn to ride Blaze, Uncle Rod's beautiful chestnut mare. I feel just like a warrior prince, he breathed, his eyes shining as he cantered around the paddock. I wish Dad could see me now.

On the last night of the holidays, Matt found himself alone in the lounge room with his mother and Sally. They were all gazing at the huge log burning in the fireplace. It was strange that the others weren't there, but Matt liked having his mother and Sally to himself. Mrs Jones came over and sat on the sofa. She got Matt to sit on one side and Sally on the other. She put her arms around them and held them close.

'I've got something to tell you two,' she began.

'Is it a story?' Sally asked, smiling across at Matt.

'Well, kind of a story, but it's really about us.'

Sally clapped her hands together. 'I like stories about us.'

'Well,' their mum began in a low voice, 'not all of this story is happy. But I think we can work out an ending that is best for all of us.'

Matt looked at his mother. 'Is this about you and Dad?'

Their mother leant over and kissed him on the top of the head and did the same to Sally. 'Darlings, Dad and I have decided to separate.'

Matt went cold. His stomach knotted.

'What does that mean?' asked Sally.

'It means that you're not going to live together, doesn't it?' Matt wanted this not to be happening. 'Why, Mum? Don't you and Dad love each other any more?'

He pulled away from his mother and stood up angrily. Sally stared from him to her mother still not fully understanding.

'Why?' Matt heard his voice getting louder and heard the tremble in it. 'What about me? Where am I going to live? You don't love me!' He felt hot stinging tears welling behind his eyes. He could hardly get the words out. 'Is this my fault? Have I done something wrong?'

'Let's be sensible about this, Matthew. You're a big boy now and we want you to finish Year Six at your school. You're enrolled in high school next year. It's a top school. Your father really wants you back with him. You can look out for each other, you know, go to footy games, see action movies, do all the boy things together.'

Matt was shaking his head.

'And you'll still be near all your friends.'

'What about Sally?'

'Sally will be staying here with me. She'll go to school with Rory and Will.'

Over and over in his head the words kept repeating, this can't be happening. 'You mean…we're all going to be split up!' Matt suddenly felt very, very tired.

They spent a long time talking and crying and eventually Sally fell asleep on her mother's lap.

'Come on.' His mother got up with Sally in her arms. 'We've had enough for one night. Let's get some sleep.'

Matt wanted to ask if he could sleep in her room. But something in the way his mother moved, the way she didn't look at him, made him hesitate.

'Mum…'

She turned, and saw in his face how difficult the evening had been for him. 'Come on, love, bring your sleeping bag into our room tonight.'

The next morning was a rush as Matt shoved clothes into his backpack, gobbled down a breakfast of eggs, toast and the last milkshake with fresh cow's milk. He thanked his uncle and aunt for having him and did high fives with his cousins. It was only when he got in the car with his mother and Sally to go to the station that the reality hit in full force. He couldn't say anything, but his mind kept going over the words his mother had said the previous night: 'Dad and I have decided to separate.'

The farewell at the station was subdued. Sally burst into tears and put her arms around him. His mother gave him a hug, but nothing like the hug that Sally had given him, which only served to confirm what Matt already had decided: Mum doesn't love me.

When he got off the train in Sydney, it was raining. He couldn't see his father and took out his phone to call.

His father came racing along the platform. 'I'm here, Matt. Couldn't find a parking spot. Crazy out there. Let's go before this storm gets any worse.' He stopped and looked at Matt. 'Country air agrees with you.' He cleared his throat. 'Everything all right up there?'

School seemed different to Matt when he started back that last term. Even the smallest things irritated him. He told Josh what his mother had said, but made him promise not to tell anyone else.

At lunchtime, Josh sat on a bench munching his sandwich. 'Aren't you going to eat your lunch?' he asked Matt.

'Nah.' Matt put his lunch down. 'Not hungry.'

'Can I have it?'

Matt nodded. Josh ate the sandwich as they sat in silence.

Then he stood up and lobbed the lunch wrapper into the bin. 'Come on, let's shoot some goals before the bell goes.

'Nah.' Matt kept staring at the ground.

Over the first week back at school, Matt's morose mood pervaded everything he did. His pat response to suggestions from Josh or any of his friends was 'Nah!'

On Friday lunchtime, Josh fronted Matt and said, 'Come to the skate park this arvo.' Josh was finding Matt difficult. 'All the guys are going after school.'

'Nah.'

'Saturday then. I'll organise a game. You'll come to that, won't you?' Josh called over his shoulder as he ran towards the basketball court.

'Maybe.' Matt looked at Josh's retreating back then returned to staring at the playground. I don't want to play basketball, Matt mused. I want Mum and Dad to get back together, for us to be a family.

The yard duty teacher strolled over. 'Not playing today, Matt? They miss you, you know.'

'Nah, miss. Don't feel like it.'

'Why don't you run along and have a game with them?'

'I said I don't want to!'

The teacher looked taken aback and the kids nearby all stopped and stared when Matt shouted. Two third graders giggled and ran off whispering to each other. The teacher nodded, turned and walked away.

Matt wished he could just disappear, get back on that dream train and go into the sky and hide behind the clouds. Everything in Matt's life was changing. He did play rehearsals, basketball training and all the other stuff, but it all felt different now. His heart wasn't in it any more.

One Sunday after lunch, there was a banging on the door. Buster hurtled down the hall, barking furiously. When Matt opened the door, Josh was standing there, basketball in hand.

'Hey, Jonesie! You up for a game?'

'Nah.'

'Hey, dude, quit moping! We need you at the park.' Josh followed Matt into the bedroom. 'You're supposed to be captain, remember?'

Matt didn't feel like doing anything. He just lay on his bed, Buster beside him.

'No! Come on, get a life!' Josh pulled Matt off the bed, ignoring both his and Buster's protests. 'I'll tell your dad we're going.'

'He doesn't care. Leave me alone!'

Josh hesitated, but there was nothing to say. As Josh left, Matt closed the bedroom door.

He flopped back on his bed and stared at the ceiling, an arm flung around Buster. He played scenes in his head, over and over again, of the great times the family had all had on holiday at the beach, or the time they went to Movie World. Days when everyone was smiling and happy. Not like now.

'I hate school,' Matt snapped at his father as they got into the car one morning. 'I want to go back to the country, to Uncle Rod's with Mum and Sally like last holidays. I hate being here.'

'You know it's best if you stay here with me, Matt. Your mother and I have agreed. We go through this every day and frankly, I'm over it.' Matt's father put his foot hard on the accelerator and the car sped off. 'You don't think it's easy for me, do you?'

'What do you mean, you've agreed?' Matt was almost shouting at his father. 'What about what I want? Does anyone think about that?' He slumped into the seat.

Mr Jones slammed on the brakes and pulled into the kerb. 'Listen, Matthew. I've had enough of this behaviour. I have to go to work and deal with grumpy people all day, then I come home to you treating me as if I am to blame for all this. I know you're upset. I am too. But we have to cope.'

He turned and looked at his son. 'I've been getting phone calls at work from your teacher telling me that you're being rude in class and getting into fights in the playground. It seems you're not doing your homework. You're nearly thirteen years old, Matthew. You're not a little kid any more.'

There was a silence as they continued on their way.

At the school gate Matt turned to his father. 'Dad, it's my birthday in three weeks. They'll come back for that, won't they?'

'Yes, of course they will. The party's organised. Now smarten up and behave yourself today. I've got to get going. See you tonight.'

A few days later, Matt found himself outside the door of the school counsellor, Miss Robson. The school principal, Mr Kavanagh, had rung Mr Jones and suggested a chat with her might help Matt with his struggles, which were showing up in poor work and what the principal described as 'uncharacteristic behavioural issues'.

Matt knocked on Miss Robson's door with some apprehension. He didn't want to see some stupid counsellor. What would everyone say when they found out about this?

At the first session, he didn't want to talk. The counsellor asked a lot of questions, but it was none of her business. She wouldn't understand anyway.

Next day, Mr Kavanagh called Matt into his office. 'Well now, how did you get on with Miss Robson?'

'All right.'

'I know it's not easy, but it does help to talk about it. I've seen you on the court. You don't give up easily, Matt. I want you to promise me one thing, that you'll go at least three more times.'

'OK.' What difference will it make anyway, he thought.

So he kept to the regular appointments. As the sessions continued, things became less difficult. Miss Robson was nice. She even asked him to call her Kathleen.

'I don't think it was your fault that your mother left. That was her choice.'

Matt puzzled over that. He had never really thought of it like that, like it was a choice thing. How do you choose to end a marriage?

Kathleen helped him see that he had choices, too. 'You can spend all weekend feeling sorry for yourself, or you can get out and have some fun. You can neglect your schoolwork and get poor marks, or you can do some work and get good results and feel proud of yourself.'

She pointed out that, if he didn't do his best at basketball practice and play rehearsals, he would be letting others down. Slowly she helped him see just how much he'd been cutting himself off from the things that made him feel good.

The bell rang as Kathleen opened the office door at the end of one session. 'See you next Friday, Matt. And, hey, happy birthday for Sunday!' She smiled at him.

'Yeah, Thanks, miss.'

'Happy birthday to you, happy birthday, dear Matt. Happy birthday to you!'

Matt's mother and Sally drove down on Friday night. They had decided to stay at Aunt Janet's, which made Matt angry. 'Why not stay with dad and me?' he had demanded down the phone. 'It's my birthday.' But his mother was quietly insistent that she and Sally couldn't stay at the house.

Matt had invited Josh and five other boys from school to his birthday party at Charlie Chuckles Crazy Diner. Charlie's was THE fun place to be, especially on your birthday, with its Big Game Adventure

Restaurant, dodgem cars, pinball parlour and fun rides on the pier jutting out over the Harbour.

Matt was amazed at the number of gifts piled up on the table when everyone was there. What his friends had bought for him was supplemented by presents from his mother and father. As he opened the gifts, Matt was awestruck. There was a new set of blades from his father and a new basketball from his mother. Josh had bought knee and elbow guards, and joked when Matt opened the present that he wanted more 'extreme' from Matt in future on the court.

Josh and the others crowded around Matt as he leant over the cake. It had been decorated to look like the skate park, with a single figure in yellow T-shirt and blades skating through the thirteen lit candles.

'You've got to make a wish when you blow them out,' the boys yelled.

He blew as hard as he could and all the candles went out, except one. It died down, then unexpectedly fluttered back into flame. The boys cheered and Matt quickly blew it out amidst much backslapping and laughter.

His mother handed him the knife to cut the cake and his father got everyone gathered around so he could take photos. Sally squeezed in next to Matt and held his hand.

'You know what I wished for, don't you?' he whispered.

She nodded.

After the party, they piled the presents into his father's car. Matt drove home with his mother, but Sally waited while her father paid the bill so she could drive home with her dad.

Buster went berserk when they all trooped into the house at the same time. Sally wanted to look at Matt's presents again as soon as they got in.

The new blades were top of the range, and Matt put them on.

Sally took a parcel from behind her back and handed it to him. 'I didn't want to give it to you at the party,' she said. 'I didn't want your friends to laugh at me. Go on, open it.' But Matt was raring to try the skates out. 'That's not fair,' she complained.

'Okay, Sal,' Matt laughed. He left the skates on and unwrapped her gift. 'Wow! *Dragon Empire* Series Two! I didn't even know it was out.'

'Why don't you have a game with Sally before we go?' His mother looked at him meaningfully.

Matt got the point and laughed. 'Okay. Dad, can we use your computer?'

Matt and Sally went into the front room and uploaded the file into the computer. Matt quickly got the hang of the game and began playing quite well.

'Come on, Sal,' he urged, 'you're not trying.'

'I am.' She looked at him. 'When are we coming home, Matt?'

'Dunno! Dad just keeps saying, "We'll have to see." Oh, nearly got a hit!'

'I want things to be the way they were.'

'Mmm. Maybe they're talking about it now. Lifeline, Sal! You're dead!'

Sally threw the control on the floor. 'I hate playing with you! You always win.'

'It's only a game, Sally.'

As they sat there in silence, they heard their parents' voices raised in argument. Sally looked at Matt in fright.

Their mother came into the room. She looked angry. 'Time to go, Sal. Sorry, Matt, we've got to get back.'

'B-but, Mum! It's my birthday!'

'Darling, I'm sorry. I'll ring you later, when we're ho…back at the farm.' She hugged him tightly, then pulled Sally to her feet. 'Come on.'

Sally was flustered. 'Do we have to go?'

Her mother held out a hand to her.

'Bye, Matt. Bye, Buster,' Sally muttered.

The dog nuzzled Sally, his tail wagging madly. Their father appeared in the doorway.

'Daddy, Daddy!' Sally burst into tears and clung to him.

'It's all right, Sal. I'll see you soon,' he murmured, hugging her.

Mrs Jones and Sally headed out the front door. Matt watched miserably as the car drove off.

He turned on his father. 'What happened? What did you say?'

'It's not what I said, son. It's what she said. Your mother wants a divorce.'

The next session with Kathleen Robson was very difficult for Matt. At first he didn't want to tell her that his parents were going to get a divorce. But when she wouldn't agree that his father had spoiled his birthday, it all came out. He finally told her everything – the arguments, his mum's note. Tears and words poured out in a jumble.

Kathleen sat quietly and listened. Eventually, Matt settled. He took the tissues she offered and wiped his face.

'It's really hard, Matt, but you have to accept your parents' decision.'

His body felt weirdly heavy and his mouth was dry. He wanted to resist what she had said, but he knew she was right. What he didn't know was what it meant to accept it.

'How about I ring your dad to come and pick you up?'

Matt nodded.

Matt was quiet over dinner that night, but when his father settled down to watch TV, Matt sat on the floor next to him.

His father looked surprised. 'You Okay, mate?'

'Yeah.'

His dad smiled and put a hand on Matt's shoulder. 'How about you teach me to play *Dragon Empire*?'

Over that weekend, they played several times and Matt was amazed at how quickly his dad cottoned on. On Sunday afternoon, his dad turned off the TV and took Matt to a movie. It was great. During the film, they pigged out on popcorn, ice cream and sweets, topped off with pizza on the way home.

On Monday after school, when Josh spotted Matt on the court holding his new basketball, he called out, 'Hey, Jonesie! Up for it?'

The other boys were happy to see Matt at the court. He was wearing the yellow T-shirt just as he used to do, and his new blades.

'Cool!' The boys were full of admiration for the new skates.

'You on my team?' Josh asked.

Matt hesitated. He'd always been captain in the past. What should he do? 'Why don't I go on the other side?'

'Wow! Fight back, eh!' The boys laughed.

'Come on,' said Josh, 'let's just do it.' He grabbed the ball from Matt and, bouncing it up and down, shouted directions at the others to get the game going. Before long, everyone was playing as hard as ever.

Matt took a fantastic intercept from Josh and bladed in to score the winning points. A smile spread across his face. 'Who's the man now!'

Josh slapped him on the shoulder. 'Great to have you back, Jonesie!'

At the end of term when the reports came out, Matt's marks were better than he had expected. And he had led his team to victory at the inter-school basketball finals. Play rehearsals had become fun again and everyone was looking forward to the performance.

On the last night of the play, as the cast took their curtain calls, the applause swept over them. The show was an enormous success and Matt was proud that he had not let them down. He beamed as he stepped forward and bowed.

In the third row, he could see his Mum, Dad and Sally grinning widely and clapping like mad. They were sitting together even though they were getting divorced. He was glad that his mother and Sally were moving back to the city.

He scanned the audience eagerly until he saw Kathleen Robson sitting with Mr and Mrs Kavanagh. She'd said she would come and he had learned to trust her.

As the curtain closed, Josh gave him a high five. 'Who's the man, Jonesie?'

The entire cast hugged one another as Mrs Beatty congratulated them all. 'I'll really miss you guys. Make the most of high school, and don't forget us!'

This story was originally conceived as a collaborative writing project with students at Hampton Community Centre.

Cat-astrophe

Moggy was an over-indulged ginger cat. She was beautiful, with a furry, ample body and dark green eyes that often glinted with malevolence. This was usually reserved for Tweetie, the German roller canary, singing in the cage just out of reach in the sitting room.

After her breakfast of Chicken Chop Supreme and Evian water, Moggy would walk noiselessly to the sitting room and spend most mornings lying in the sun on the red and green tartan chaise longue, dreaming of one day having canary for breakfast. The chaise stood under the sitting room window, which was perfect for viewing the passing parade. However, she did have to put up with Tweetie whistling and showing off her throaty rolling warbles for minutes on end. That was when Moggy's green eyes became slitted and at their most danger-ous-looking. That was when her claws would come out and she would scratch at the fabric covering the chaise.

Moggy's owner, Mrs Muddleson, had never got round to reuphol-stering the chaise, which had many tears where Moggy had clawed at the fabric, shredding it. Moggy calculated that if Tweetie kept whistling and she kept clawing at the fabric, Mrs Muddleson one day soon would have to reupholster the whole thing.

Under the sitting room window was Moggy's favourite place to lie. Beside the curved back end of the chaise was a tall Kentia palm in a tarnished brass pot. Moggy loved to lie on her back and stretch up to those seemingly shredded leaves. How lovely it would be to feel her claws cutting through those slender strips. How lovely it would be to feel her claws cutting into yellow feathers. However, the palm leaves were too high and so was Tweetie. Moggy would tire quickly of this game and roll over to watch the comings and goings on the street.

She was always delighted to see those absurdly ridiculous four-legged misfits, the local dogs, panting and prancing, barking and slobbering on leashes tugged along by their appalling owners. Appalling owners because only silly creatures would stoop to own something as grotesque as a dog. Mrs Muddleson would never stoop so low. She was an aesthete and the cat was the pinnacle of beauty, grace and cuddly comfort.

Mrs Muddleson adored Moggy and Moggy reciprocated by treating her mistress with a level of distain verging on contempt. Despite this, Moggy had to admit that the mistress was useful for things like making breakfast, emptying the kitty litter tray and washing the blankets that lined the cat basket.

One bright autumn day, Mrs Muddleson was doing her weekly cleaning of the house. Moggy shot an irritated glance at the vacuum cleaner and knew that its frightful noise would soon destroy the pleasure of her morning. When that machine started, she always walked pointedly out of the room, refusing to be cajoled by Mrs Muddleson's apologies for disturbing her.

Moggy took these opportunities to go into the garden where she would hide in bushes, waiting for an unsuspecting sparrow to land on the lawn or a skink to scurry onto the pavers and sun itself. Her eyes would narrow, her body would tense low to the ground and her tail would stand straight out from her hind legs stiff as an arrow. She would bide her time, then, at the right moment, pounce. Those mornings were a highlight in her otherwise sedentary existence.

On this day, crouched as she was in the garden under a hydrangea bush, she heard the phone ring. The vacuum cleaner stopped and she heard Mrs Muddleson's voice. After a short burst of human meowing, she heard Mrs Muddleson go back into the living room. She could hear the sounds of that awful machine being hauled back into the storage cupboard in the hall. Then she heard Tweetie's cage being cleaned and Mrs Muddleson walking into the kitchen with the soiled paper that had been used to line the bottom of the cage.

At last, Moggy thought. You seemed to take forever today to clean the room. You're getting older, she purred, taking longer to do simple tasks. Most annoying!

Now I can go back to my post-prandial rest, she thought. The phone rang again, but Moggy ignored the sound of Mrs Muddleson's hurrying back to the kitchen and continued on her way with unharried dignity. Who'd be a human? she thought.

In the living room, as she sprang heavily onto the chaise longue, she saw something wonderful. It was the most amazing sight she had ever seen in this room. Possibilities bloomed in her feline mind, the kind of possibility of which she had only ever dreamed before. Longing, desire and ancient instincts came together as she saw that the gate to Tweetie's cage was open and the canary had come out into the room and was sitting on a curtain rod.

Moggy didn't have to think what to do. She flattened herself on the tattered fabric of the chaise and slowly tensed her body, watching.

Flying from one side of the room to another, Tweetie was chirping with excitement, but baulked at going through the door into the dark of the hallway. She landed on the bureau and hopped onto the bookshelves. As she explored the room, she flew ever lower and lower.

Moggy's eyes glowed with a malevolent intent, eyes the colour of dark jade that comes from the depths of extinct volcanoes. Tweetie landed on the Kentia palm which bent a little under her weight, down towards the chaise longue. The cat drew herself up to spring as Mrs Muddleson came back into the room, saw that was about to happen and screamed.

Tweetie flew up to the curtain rod, Moggy collapsed back onto the chaise longue with an infuriated howl. Then Mrs Muddleson was chasing Moggy around the room, shrieking at her until Moggy fled through the door and found a place to hide at the back of the house.

Mrs Muddleson closed the living room door, shutting Moggy out. She coaxed Tweetie back into her cage with fresh seed and a slice of apple brought specially from the kitchen. How wounding to a cat's pride was that, that the mistress would privilege a prattling yellow pip-squeak over a superior being like Moggy.

Things were never the same after that day. Tweetie went on singing superbly at the living room window, earning praise from passers-by. The window was now left open on warm days as there was no Moggy on the chaise longue to escape through it into the front garden with its abundance of wildlife. The chaise longue was reupholstered in a beautiful fabric featuring spring flowers overlaying a jacquard lattice pattern. The faded curtains were replaced with a simple, pale moss drill and the kentia palm was repotted and the brass container polished to a brilliant glow.

Moggy never saw these changes. She was banished to the back of the house. Her cat basket was moved into the laundry and she was put on a no-name cat food diet. Moggy was fiercely resentful of these changes and did her best to shred any washing that was left hanging out of the basket on top of the washing machine.

But she did have one compensation. And that was the memory of the wonderful primeval surge of hunting instincts that had pro-pelled her heavy-bodied bulk up towards that blasted yellow canary. She understood from that day on that she belonged to a proud line of hunters who knew how to track down prey and how to kill – well, almost how to kill.

Soiled, Foiled and Frisked

This must be the worst day of my life. One of the worst. How on earth have I got myself into this bloody mess?

Geraint St John Aldrich, CEO, philanthropist, major contributor to the conservative side of politics and a pillar of society, stood with his palms flat against the greasy wall of the diner and his legs apart as a young constable felt up the legs of his trousers and rubbed his perineum between his balls and his bum.

My legendary namesakes wouldn't have put up with any of this, he thought, as old bookish images of the Welsh king and Arthurian knight rose in his mind. This young cop would have been impaled on a pike and posted at the sliding doors of this dump.

'Don't move.' The young constable's voice was riding on the assumption of power that his uniform gave him.

Geraint wanted to tell him he was a nothing, a mere foot soldier in the great chronicle of keeping the King's peace.

Earlier that morning, Geraint had got up, shaved and showered while Edie, his wife, got breakfast for the kids downstairs. He'd gone to his underpants drawer and stared in frustration at its emptiness. All his underpants were in the laundry basket, soiled, waiting for him to put on a wash. 'Bugger,' he'd sworn.

The lack of clean underpants was the result of his failure to carry out his side of a domestic demarcation dispute settlement between him and Edie. 'Tough love' she had called it when she set down the terms of household responsibilities that they were to share. He could hear her now carrying out her major tasks, feeding the kids and getting them off to school. A reciprocal duty of his was to do the laundry and he had already failed twice in recent weeks: Ambrose's soccer gear had lain in the clothes basket, smelling out the laundry, and there'd been no clean school blouse for Daisy on Tuesday. Both kids had ranted at him as if he had committed a corporate crime while Edie rang her sister to borrow her children's clean clothes. The ensuing rush to get everything ready had ended in a shouting match between him and Edie and a slammed front door.

'I can't not wear underpants,' he fumed. Ambrose! But his son had the slender, powerful hips of a fifteen-year-old sports fanatic. I'll never get into them. Either I'll rip them or go through the day speaking in a falsetto. I have to be comfortable, especially today of all days.

Edie!

He went to his wife's drawer. Full to the brim. How come, he puzzled, her knickers are clean and mine aren't? Nonetheless, Edie's full drawer had soothed his irritation and offered a solution. He fossicked through the knickers, looking for a plain and simple pair. However, Edie didn't do plain and simple, as he knew from years of being turned on by seeing her in lingerie.

He'd picked up a pair of pale pink knickers with grey lace trim around the legs and an embroidered rose. Holding on to them, he'd rummaged through the drawer once more, but decided to stick to the pink and grey as he heard the kids calling out goodbye and the front door slam shut. Edie would be in the bedroom in a minute. He hoisted himself into the knickers and quickly pulled on his suit pants just as she entered the bedroom.

'Why is my drawer open?' she'd demanded.

His mind was on guard against just such an attack. He grabbed a shirt from his side of the wardrobe and replied, 'Checking you're all right for underwear. I'll put on a wash before I go.'

'I've just put one on, Geri. A bargain is a bargain and you're not holding up your end. Not good enough.' With that comment, Edie went into the bathroom and closed the door.

Geraint had breathed a sigh of relief as he heard the shower turn on.

Although it was half an hour before he needed to leave, Geraint couldn't get out of the house quickly enough. I'll pick up a coffee and something to eat on the way, he decided.

Once on the main road, he swung into the right hand lane and was met with a blast from a tradie. 'Bugger!' he muttered, looking away from the angry tradie's face in the rear-vision mirror. I haven't done anything wrong, so why do I feel guilty? Is it because I haven't done the laundry or because I'm wearing a pair of Edie's panties? Maybe I should have told her. Whatever. There's no way I'm going to be comfortable in these, he thought, shifting in the seat, trying to ease the constraining tightness of the undies.

I'll get close to Blacktown, call in to a roadside diner and pick up a coffee and toasty, Geraint thought. I can't go to this important meeting on an empty stomach. The final details of the proposed merger have to be nutted out and agreed to before the proposal can be put to the shareholders. We're almost over the line with this one, so I have to be on the ball.

He had been driving for about twenty-five minutes when his phone rang. It was Edie. He answered and asked her to wait while he pulled over. He spied a diner attached to a service station and drove in and parked. Heads turned to look at the gleaming Mercedes, so out of place alongside the battered ute, the Toyota Supra and hotted up Mazda RX-7. Geraint hesitated for a moment. This kind of place is an excrescence, he thought. Don't want to eat anything here. I'll just get a coffee and get one of the girls at the office to get me something to eat. They won't mind.

'Edie.'

He listened while Edie railed against him for leaving without saying goodbye, for not doing the laundry, for not putting her drawer back, for not…

'What kind of a marriage is this?' she demanded.

He sat poker-faced while she vented her grievance at him. Then he apologised, promising to reform and do better next time. He made a mental note to get one of the girls back in head office to pick up a big bunch of flowers for him to take home that night. He had rung off with a 'Love you.'

'Coffee, coffee, coffee,' he mouthed repeatedly, step-by-step as he walked towards the smell of over-cooked and stale foods seeping out of the sliding doors of the diner. He waited his turn to be served, enjoying the incongruity of his Ermenegildo Zegna suit and Rockport Allander shoes compared to the scruffy jeans and T-shirts of the other customers.

Everything about him was attracting attention. He didn't mind the stares. In his mind they recognised he was a cut above them. He knew he was wealthier than these people, was better dressed and altogether had a better life than them. I'm more at ease with them than they are with me, he mused. The point is, I work hard for what I have. That's what it's about.

He had just ordered his coffee when the roar of motorbikes pulling up outside was a raucous fanfare turning heads, quickening the pulse and sending a couple of customers scurrying out of the diner. Geraint turned to look out the window and saw five bikies. The roar of engines died and the bikies got off their machines, took off their helmets. They sauntered over to his Mercedes and started scrutinising it.

You do anything to it and I'll have you in court before you know it, Geraint thought, watching, waiting in case one of them tried anything with the car.

One big bruiser of a man looked into the diner, catching Geraint's eye. Geraint held the man's gaze, aware the two of them were taking stock of each other through the window. The bikie was an anomaly beside the gleaming Mercedes, but he emanated the aura of a prince of power leading his squad of hardened riders. Often, Geraint had seen gangs of bikies cruise past on highways, in the mountains and down the coast, but he had never been so close to a gang as this.

Geraint turned back to the owner who was watching the bikies. 'Long black, no sugar,' he repeated.

The bikies pushed into the diner. They stood in a line behind the big guy, clearly their leader, who was appraising Geraint with a taut smile on his face.

The man behind the counter jerked his head back in acknowledgement of a signal from one of the bikies and spoke in a high nasal tone. 'Thought youse were gonna be 'ere early.'

'Morning, Deep Fry. Miss me, did you?' One of the bikies stepped forward and slid a parcel across the counter to Deep Fry, who quickly grabbed it and put it behind a stack of chocolate-coated candy bars. He handed the bikie a bulging envelope.

Geraint's instincts told him to forego the coffee and get out of the diner now. He turned and was facing a line of unshaven, tough-looking, denim-wearing, tattooed men with close-cropped hair and boots that looked fit to kick heads.

It had been a very long time since Geraint had felt intimidated, not since he was one of the young Turks in the corporate world. He was feeling the return of old memories of unease at being dressed down by company directors, the humiliation of being patronised by personal assistants and office managers. Now those long-forgotten feelings were threatening to return in force.

'Nice bit of hardware you've got out there,' the lead bikie said, running his eyes insolently over Geraint.

Geraint turned, surprised by the fine timbre of the big guy's voice. It flashed into Geraint's mind that the bikie sounded like a private-school boy, not western suburbs state high school, not like Deep Fry. The two men perused each other. Geraint sensed that they were jumping to conclusions from first impressions, both admiring the stature, the proud stance of the other while becoming wary of each other at the same time.

They were of roughly equal height and similar stature, but clearly princes of separate domains. The one a captain of industry, a minister of finance and the entrepreneur of daring business ventures. The other a captain of the demimonde, a chancellor of the black economy and a mastermind of subterfuge.

'Nice car, nice suit, nice shoes.' The bikie's voice drawled with bare-ly concealed contempt. 'Upstanding citizen, eh?'

'I like expensive things,' Geraint replied matter-of-factly.

There was a ripple of mockery among the other bikies. 'Oh, do you now?' the big bikie sneered.

There it is again, after all these years, Geraint thought. Same old, same old put-down tone. Who are you to speak to me like that? 'Not all of us look good in old denim and worn leather.' He saw the bikie bridle at this, but Geraint had regained his confidence and wanted to face down the bullying tone.

His eyes narrowed and he ran them deliberately over the big guy. It surprised him how good-looking he was under the unshaven face and grimy clothes. He almost laughed out loud at the thought of offering to wash the bikie's clothes with his dirty underpants.

He let his eyes turn to look out the window at the bike the big guy was riding. He kept his eyes on the bike as he spoke. 'I wouldn't wear your kind of clothes,' Geraint said, 'but you do have a sense of style… bikie style. Your jacket is good-quality leather, a bit battered, but it fits you well. Though it's the Kawasaki GPZ900R that is the thing that really interests me about you.'

Geraint looked back at the big guy just in time to see him wipe the surprise off his face. He liked that, catching people out with his unexpected knowledge.

'It's a good bit of hardware.' Geraint emphasised the word hardware to press home that he had noticed the sarcasm about his Mercedes. 'I wouldn't have picked you as a man of nostalgia.' He paused, holding the big guy's stare. 'That's the bike Tom Cruise chose to ride in *Top Gun 1*. That machine was ahead of its time in the 1980s and is still a good performer. Fancy yourself as a bit of a Tom Cruise Top Gun, do you?'

Geraint heard the undertone of mockery in his voice, knew what he had said was provocative and realised that he had probably made a mistake saying anything at all. He wasn't used to being tactful to underlings, but this wasn't head office and the bikie facing him certainly wasn't an underling, at least not to him. Just leave, he told himself and moved to step past the big guy.

'Cancel the coffee,' he said over his shoulder to Deep Fry and took a step towards the door.

The bikie's face darkened. He took a menacing step forward. 'We don't like smart-arse dudes around here, do we, boys?'

For an instant, Geraint heard himself uttering those same words to some young bloke in the office after he'd made an inappropriate interjection or some flippant remark. Bit ironic, he reflected.

There was a flurry of agreement among the bikies.

'Fuckin' city wankers,' one of the gang snarled.

The two men were now standing close to each other. The bikie dropped a backpack to the ground between him and Geraint. Straddling the backpack, he fingered Geraint's lapels, folding the fabric in his fingers, all the time tightening his grip on the jacket. In a sudden action, the bikie tried to pull Geraint closer. Geraint pushed back with his hand on the other man's chest. There was a mocking whoop from the other bikies, which acted on Geraint to make him acutely conscious of the hard muscles under his palm.

'What do you think you're doing?' Geraint snapped. 'Let go.'

Outside, the roar of traffic seemed to have reached a crescendo. Something was going on out there, but Geraint dare not take his eyes off the bikie for fear of being set upon without warning. His mind was racing, trying to remember moves of attack and escape. He had never been a fighter. There had been the usual scraps over handball in lower primary school and scrimmages at rugby matches, but never anything serious. Never anything like this.

The only thought in his mind now was that if he didn't leave, he was going to be beaten up. Geraint was strongly built, worked out regularly and played squash. But he knew he wasn't going to be a match for this gorilla – gorilla and support pack. Face-to-face and with perspiration seeping under his armpits, he needed to come to terms with the man destroying the lapels of his suit, his two-and-a-half-thousand-dollar suit. Under the stubble, under the dirt-smeared, weathered skin he was struck again by the man's good looks.

Violence, the apprehension of violence, was oppressing Geraint's mind, trying to sidetrack it into safer territory, into a place where he was familiar with using his aura of authority, his good looks and charm to get his own way. It struck him that this bikie wasn't stupid. His eyes blazed with a malevolent intelligence as he thrust into Geraint's panic, pulling him so close that their lips were almost touching.

'Pretty boy, smell good' Geraint heard as his knees went weak with fear.

'Why are we doing this?' Geraint heard his voice strong and resonant, the voice of a powerful CEO questioning underlings. His eyes widened at the sound and he was eyeballing the bikie.

There was a hiatus of surprise as disbelief spread across the bikie's face. Geraint wanted to reason with the man who possessed those eyes, that skin, those lips. Surely this man would respond to reason, wouldn't he?

'Cops! Fuckin' cops!' Deep Fry was yelling as he grabbed the parcel from behind the confectionery display and bolted for the back door, running straight into two policemen entering through it.

'I'll take that,' one of the officers said and snatched the parcel from Deep Fry.

Geraint was disoriented as the diner was suddenly swarming with police, armed police pointing guns and shouting, 'Hands against the wall! Hands against the wall! Now, do it!'

Geraint stepped around the backpack and headed for the door.

'No you don't, sweetheart,' a solidly built, ruddy-faced officer snapped, stepping in front of Geraint and placing a foot on the backpack. 'Against the wall with your mates. Hands on the wall. Legs apart. Do it. Now.'

'I'm not with them,' Geraint stammered. 'I'm a businessman. I'm going to a meeting. I don't know these men.'

'I'll say it one more time. Hands against the wall, legs apart, now.'

Geraint felt all his limbs go heavy. He moved like an automaton and found himself standing next to a bikie with his hands on the wall. It took some moments for his mind to unlock and his speech to return. He looked around, searching for someone else who might be in command. But it was the ruddy-faced sergeant who was shouting orders to the other police and Geraint guessed it must be him.

Raising his voice over the noise of the ruckus, he called to the sergeant. 'Let me use my phone. I can prove I'm not with them. My phone. In my jacket pocket.' Geraint moved his hand up to the inner pocket of his jacket.

'Don't move!'

Geraint's request was ignored as the sergeant ordered his men to frisk the bikies. Geraint closed his eyes in disbelief, but opened them suddenly as he felt a pair of hands inserted under his armpits and begin working down his ribs, over his buttocks, between his legs and continue down the inner thighs and over the calves. Then the probing went into reverse as the hands began moving up the front of his legs, across his hips and crotch.

This has got to be the worst day of my life, Geraint thought. Then the constable flicked his balls and Geraint gasped at the stab of pain that ran through him.

'Don't move,' the young constable ordered.

The frisking continued over his belly, waist and chest. Somewhere along the way, Geraint realised that the constable frisking him was feeling the lining of his jacket. At first Geraint thought it was to ascertain if there was anything hidden in the lining. However, the movement continued. The officer's fingers were rubbing the fabric, feeling…feeling what? For God's sake, Geraint thought, he's feeling the quality of the cloth. He turned and saw a fresh-faced young man standing behind him. The young constable grinned and mouthed the words, 'Nice suit.'

Geraint was completely nonplussed, not knowing whether his part in this was for real or a farce. He stared at the young constable, unsure whether to smile back or nod or tell him to piss off and let him go. His phone rang and he reached for it inside his jacket.

'I told you not to move,' the sergeant yelled from across the diner.

'This will be important,' Geraint insisted, but the sergeant glared at him, unflinching.

The phone stopped ringing. A few seconds later, there was the ping of a message coming in.

'Sarge, got something here,' one of the officers called from further down the line.

The sergeant put on rubber gloves and took a plastic bag from the constable and examined the contents. The room had gone quiet as the other officers craned their necks to see what was in the bag.

Then the sergeant handed the bag to one of his team. 'Mark it up for evidence.' 'Get gloves for everyone,' he ordered.

There was a groan from some of the constables and an expletive shot out through the room from one of the bikies. 'Body cavity search,' the sergeant ordered.

Geraint sensed a hint of glee in the command.

'You're fuckin' kiddin',' the head bikie snarled.

'No way,' another snapped.

'Strip!' the sergeant commanded. 'Do it.'

None of the bikies moved.

'Now!' The sergeant bellowed. 'Strip.'

Amidst a growing swell of the foulest language Geraint had ever heard, first one, then another of the bikies began to obey. Soon they were all dropping their jackets, T-shirts, jeans and boots on the floor behind them. There was a routine about the stripping which made Geraint think that it wasn't the first time these men had been asked to do this.

The phone rang again. Geraint reached into his jacket, but the sergeant was beside him, pulling his jacket open and taking the phone.

'You too, your lordship.' The sergeant leaned in, his eyes narrowed and his jaw set. 'Strip.'

'For God's sake,' Geraint began. 'I've already told you, I'm a businessman. Let me show you my business card. Let me phone my lawyer.'

'Let me repeat it one more time,' the sergeant said. 'Strip.'

Geraint paled. I can't, he thought. I'm wearing Edie's knickers. No, no, this can't be happening. He opened his mouth to speak, but the look on the sergeant's face and the confusion around him made him realise it was pointless. His phone rang again. 'That'll be Tom, my 2IC,' he said, 'wondering where I am. If you answer the phone you'll see…'

The sergeant ignored him, turned and walked down the line barking orders to his men.

Geraint took off his jacket, folded it and looked around for somewhere to place it. The jacket was grabbed from him and thrown onto the floor. Dread mounted as he undid his tie, unbuttoned his shirt and took off his shoes and socks. Then he baulked.

There was a cry of pain down the line. Geraint turned to see one of the bikies bent over with a gloved finger inserted in his rear end. They can't do this, he repeated over and over in his mind. I won't let them do this to me.

'Bingo, Sarge!' An officer was holding a plastic packet which he had extracted from the bikie's rectum.

It was quickly followed by another constable holding up a packet, saying, 'Got another here!'

'Foiled again,' a constable sneered somewhere down the line. 'When are you dopy pricks ever going to learn?'

Geraint was appalled by the grotesque scene that was unfolding around him. Then he felt a hand slam into his back, forcing his head against the wall. Pain shot through his cheekbone and jaw. They began to throb.

Geraint's phone rang again and the sergeant swore. He gave the phone to the young constable standing beside him and snapped, 'Turn the bloody thing off. Put it in a bag and mark it up.'

Geraint's heart sank. That was his lifeline to the outside world and it was now cut off.

'Well, well, what are you hiding, your lordship?'

Everyone was now watching the sergeant and Geraint.

'Get dressed!' the sergeant yelled down the line.

The bikies moved as one, reaching down for their clothes. To Geraint, the movement looked almost choreographed, totally out of keeping with the point of view that he had that bikies were anarchic and dangerous. It wasn't as if he hadn't seen men getting dressed before. Changing rooms at the gym, the squash courts, the swimming pool were all full of men getting changed, getting dressed. But none of those situations were like this where the bikies, who were usually feared, were acting like an obedient chorus line, pulling on their costumes, ready for the next act – at the police station.

'Pants and underpants,' was all the sergeant said to Geraint, but the way he said it brooked no objection.

Geraint felt numb.

'Are you going to do what I told you or do I have to get my boys to turn you upside down?'

Geraint rested his forehead on the wall, willing it to wrap around and absorb him, make him disappear. Most of the bikies were already dressed and were looking in his direction, waiting to see how the confrontation between Geraint and the sergeant panned out.

There was no way out of it. He was going to have to strip completely. It was with mounting dread that Geraint undid his belt. With fingers trembling, he undid the buttons on the waistband of his trousers and slid down the zip of his fly. He hesitated, hoping for a miracle to happen, that someone would walk into the diner and order the police to stop. But it didn't happen and with eyes closed, Geraint let his trousers drop to the floor.

The CEO on his way to an important and expensive merger that had taken two years of negotiations to bring to fruition stood in the shabby diner in his wife's pink briefs with the grey lace trim. He was flushed and sweating, a light-headedness threatening to unbalance him. Geraint was painfully aware of all the aspects of his manhood bulging uncomfortably through the thin fabric as a stunned silence battered his eardrums. He cast a quick glance at the head bikie and cringed at the bemused look on his face. No, Geraint wanted to shout. I can explain. This is not a thing, not something I do.

Thump, thump, thump! It wasn't the pulse of silence marking the time. It was his heart racing to get out of his chest and hide somewhere. He thought with a sense of horror that the only thing now standing between him and an internal search wasn't the hope of a miracle, but a strip of flimsy fabric that barely covered his arse.

The astonished silence was quickly broken by a shrill wolf whistle. This was followed by roars of laughter, shouts of 'kinky!' and catcalls. The bikie beside him puckered his lips and moved his tongue in and out while a volley of obscene comments shot back and forth from both sides of the criminal divide in the diner. Geraint saw the hard, unsmiling stare of the head bikie and he turned back to the wall.

The sergeant set about restoring some semblance of order. He instructed an officer to call for a paddy wagon and tell the station to get ready to receive the bikies. He told them they were being taken to the police station where they would be charged with drug offences.

The sergeant stood close to Geraint examining him, eyes narrowed, lips drawn tightly together. 'Well, well, your ladyship,' he drawled. 'Get off on that kind of thing, do you?'

Everyone was now watching the sergeant and Geraint.

'Underpants,' the sergeant snapped, 'or do you prefer panties?'

Geraint dropped the undies to the floor. In a way he felt better, standing naked, freed from the shame of Edie's knickers. He felt a hand push him back to the wall and boots forcing his legs apart. He glanced again at the lead bikie. Now Geraint was the only man in the diner without his clothes on. Nakedness, the great leveller, he thought.

Time became suspended as he stood waiting for the final bit of this indignity to take place. Who's the big man now? he thought, glancing back at the head bikie. Two leaders at the top of their games reduced to this, reduced to the lowest common denominator.

He had no idea how long he stood there, sounds and voices becoming no more than white noise as he blocked out the rest of the diner and the impending body cavity search. Then slowly he became aware of something taking place, something that wasn't an internal body search. Voices were yelling outside and the officers in the diner were talking all at once. The sergeant's voice came from the sliding doors which had opened, letting in the roar of traffic on the highway. Feeling disembodied and drained of will, Geraint convinced himself he could hear the voice of Tom, calling his name. Wishful thinking, he deduced.

'Get dressed.'

Who said that? Who is talking to me? Is that you, Tom? Geraint dared to turn round and saw the young constable standing next to him.

'Get dressed,' he urged.

Geraint didn't move. He felt he was hallucinating, seeing Tom and Leon, his company executives, outside arguing with the sergeant, surrounded by a ring of police.

'Get dressed,' the young constable repeated, more urgently.

Geraint reached down and eased himself into Edie's pink and grey lace undies. He had picked up his trousers when the crowd of police at the door parted and he saw Tom and Leon coming towards him. Geraint saw them hesitate, disbelief on their faces as they stared at the pink knickers. Then Geraint snapped back into CEO mode. He pulled on his trousers, got into his shoes, put on his shirt and redid the tie.

As he pulled on his jacket, he remembered the phone. He turned to the young constable. 'My phone. The sergeant took it.' As the officer moved to retrieve it, Geraint looked at Tom. 'How did you find me?'

Tom cleared his throat, freeing up his voice and clearing away the embarrassment he felt. 'You were late. You're never late. We tracked you on the phone. You seemed stuck here, you weren't answering the phone and we decided you'd had an accident or something. So we hot-footed it down here to check out what was going on.'

The young constable gave Geraint his phone and Geraint moved to the door. He stopped in front of the sergeant and turned to look at the bikies. The lead guy was standing, staring defiantly at Geraint's exit. Then he gave a slight nod, enough for Geraint to notice and return the gesture. The communication was strange, enigmatic and unsettling. Maybe it's some kind of recognition of my being let off the hook but him not. Maybe he thinks we're more like each other than not. Or is that what I think?

Two princes, Geraint thought, two different pathways, two different outcomes, two different men. As his eyes lingered on the bikie, he continued to wonder about what it was that made the difference between them. Those differences began long before this morning, I guess. But I'm not so very different from the bikie once you take off the clothes and are standing butt naked surrounded by a cluster of uniformed police. The levelling effect of nudity, Geraint thought, and the levelling effect of uniforms. The levelling effect of being ensnared in the justice system.

These cops wield power like it's personal. It's not. It's state power, but they use it like personal power. The image of the naked bikies rose again in his mind. Even without clothes, they looked frightening with their tattoos, their grey ponytails and plaits. Cops use violence, pushing us against the wall, pushing my head into the wall, shoving their hands inside our bodies. Get the clothes off and you're a blip, an outsider, a loser. Keep the uniform on and you have the power that goes with it. But the uniform makes you forget just how much you are a small cog in a very big, complex wheel.

Geraint's mind shifted away from all the maddening details of the morning. What about me and power? I boss people around at work and expect them to do as I ask. Am I like that with Edie and the kids? Has the bossiness trickled over into the home? Does a policeman's use of violence spill over into his private life? Are we all stuffed by the work we do?

He turned to the sergeant. 'You made a big mistake with me. Not everybody in a set of circumstances is there for the same reason. If policing can't distinguish between the real culprits and people who happen to be caught up in the circumstances, then God help us.'

He walked in silence with Tom and Leon to the car. He felt a heaviness, a sluggishness descending on him and realised his hands were trembling. He put them in his pockets.

Tom looked at him sideways. 'All right?' he asked.

'I'll drive your car,' Leon said.

'I'm fine,' Geraint answered. He didn't notice the two men exchange glances.

'I agree you shouldn't drive,' Tom cut in. 'You need to chill.'

Geraint got into Tom's car and settled back into the plush leather seat. He wanted to sleep, but his mind kept on working. How am I going to explain this? he thought. Everything has changed and nothing has changed.

When they arrived at the Penrith offices where the meeting was to be held, Leon got one of the staff to go out and buy breakfast for Geraint. Tom settled Geraint in the boardroom and suggested that he, Tom, chair the meeting. Geraint demurred, but he knew that Tom was right. There was no way he could hold it together, arguing detailed points of an agreement with the executives of the other company.

Tom did take charge of the meeting, with Geraint sitting at the head of the table like an aloof emperor or pontiff, quietly nodding his assent or shaking his head in disagreement.

Geraint couldn't put the morning's events out of his mind. The appalling image of the naked bikies flowed in and out of the meeting, their bare backsides with gloved hands probing, the occasional cry of pain and the laughter of the police.

He couldn't dismiss the conundrum of the head bikie. How did a man like that turn out so badly? he wondered. Man like that? Like what? Everything about that man is based on the assumptions I made, snap impressions that arose from the confrontation when we first came face to face in the diner. He could be a total arsehole for all I know.

But I'm sure I'm right. He's like me. No! It's the other way round. I'm more like him. We're both leaders, both run businesses, both manage a team of underlings, both know when to be ruthless…and we were both curious about the other. No one else there wondered who I was or what I was doing there. The sergeant made his own assumptions – if I was in the diner with a group of bikies, then I must be with them, must be somehow involved with them, on the wrong side of the law.

By lunchtime, Geraint felt he had exhausted all the possibilities about the morning, the head bikie, the police raid and the pernicious persistence of the memory of his standing against the wall in his wife's knickers. He still couldn't make sense of his preoccupation with the details that kept zeroing into his mind – the young cop's nastiness in flicking his balls then feeling the quality of his suit; the belligerence of the sergeant and his refusal to listen when Geraint tried to explain who he was; the passive compliance of the bikies with the police orders to strip and bend over; the raucous reaction when he dropped his trousers to the floor.

Tom and Leon had both seen him like that when he started to get dressed. They would remember that, probably talk about him in private, wonder whether he always wore women's underwear. Would the incident change things between them? Will my authority as CEO now be compromised even if I try to explain it to them? How can I explain it – Tom, Leon, I don't wear women's underwear. It was just a crazy set of circumstances. I didn't have a clean pair of underpants, so I grabbed a pair of Edie's. Stupid as that might seem, that's what happened. My mistake. I hadn't done the laundry. That's my job at home. I grabbed her knickers, got dressed and got out of the house while Edie was in the bathroom. I was embarrassed. And I hadn't had breakfast, you see, but my little plan for a takeaway breakfast got foiled when the bikies turned up at that diner, then the police. Then I had to strip like everyone else.

At the end of the day, the merger had been finalised, but Geraint's comprehension of the details would have to wait until he read the minutes and talked to Tom and Leon. He had been an absent presence for most of the meeting.

Geraint reassured everyone that he was fit to drive and set off home. Edie and the kids were already there when he drove into the garage.

As soon as he walked into the house, Daisy ran up to him. 'Daddy, what happened to your face?'

Geraint mumbled an excuse about banging into a door. Edie scrutinised him, but said nothing, not believing him. Ambrose said he looked as if he had been in a fight. He got through dinner relatively as normal, though Ambrose kept asking him why he was being so weird and demanded to know if he had been in a fight.

After the dinner things had been cleared away and the kids went to their rooms, Geraint poured Edie and himself a glass of port and sat down with her.

'Edie, there's something I have to tell you. No, please don't interrupt and no, I'm not having an affair, nothing like that. It's about something that happened this morning on the way to Penrith. Well, actually it began before I left this morning.'

Edie sat stony-faced, rotating the glass of port on the coaster beside her chair.

'Remember when you came into the bedroom this morning and asked why your underwear drawer was open…?'

Tet

'Cuc mung nam moi!' The words of the New Year greeting were emblazoned in gold letters on a long red banner stretching across the entire width of the vestibule. The din of excited chatter flowed out from the large eating salon, carried on the mouth-watering aroma of spicy food, spreading like a second atmosphere throughout the space. The head waiter's round face beamed as the group walked into the restaurant for the New Year's Eve celebration.

Duong Vo hung back at the rear of the tour party, where she had been trailing the other members since they had attended the official Tet memorial ceremony in a town square. Suited men, party apparatchiks and senior bureaucrats, had made up the official party. No women, she noted with distain. This promise of the war against the imperialists had not been fulfilled but the speeches were long, self-congratulatory and full of bullshit. They had been in Ho Chi Minh City for two days and she didn't like it. In fact, by the end of the first day, she was regretting that she had allowed her daughter Hoang to talk her into coming on a tour to Vietnam for the Tet holiday.

Even before she had boarded the Air Vietnam flight, Duong Vo was wondering at what point she could dump the tour group. Her doubts about the trip began at Sydney airport with an ex-major from the former South Vietnamese army who somehow picked her as an oddity. Being from the North and living in Sydney amongst communities from the South had accustomed her to being the odd one out. 'She's a snob,' they'd say. 'Prefers to live on the North Shore rather than among her own people.' 'My people!' Duong Vo sneered to herself. It my people who fight each other in war. My people, both sides who commit most horrific atrocities on each other. Aided by cynical allies. Viet people kill my brother and father just as I kill other brothers and fathers. What about Australians be my people now. Your people, our people? Australia our country now.

When people were introducing themselves at the beginning of the tour the self-proclaimed major had assumed a leadership role which annoyed Duong Vo. Let him be the big man, she thought, but when he had introduced himself as a former major it soured her feelings towards him. Not the fact that they had fought on opposite sides, but that he was posturing in front of the others, demanding a higher status, expecting deferential treatment and getting it. All the reasons we fought them, Duong Vo had thought, watching him carry on about the courageous South leadership from Ngo Dinh Dimh to Ng Van Min.

There was one woman who befriended Mrs Vo on the second day of the tour. They were at the old Chinese market in Cholon, which was chaotic with people buying food and gifts for the holiday. The ex-major was carrying on about the old days of the South Vietnam Republic and how this market had been a place of intrigue and espionage.

Mrs Nguyen turned to Mrs Vo and said quietly without a smile, 'I am surprised that he was never sold here as the baboon that he is. I could have got a high price for him.'

Mrs Vo was shocked that the woman had picked her as being of similar opinion and that she understood her enough on such short acquaintance to speak like that. Her face showed no response. Am I that transparent? she wondered with a little alarm. Then a smile crept across her face and she held a handkerchief to her nose to hide it. Mrs Nguyen nodded and let a smile twinkle her eyes.

The third and last day in Ho chi Minh City was New Year's Day. The city was deserted as Mrs Vo slipped out of the hotel early.

A taxi was waiting at the kerb and she got in, showing the driver a piece of paper with an address written on it. 'Do you know this place?' she asked.

The driver read and reread the address, frowned and nodded. He looked at her in the rear-vision mirror and shook his head. 'Bad part of town,' he said as he started the engine and the car moved off.

They drove for some time through mainly deserted streets passing buildings which became shabbier and shabbier as they went. The emptiness was unsettling, but she knew that Tet was a time when people travelled in droves over long distances to spend the New Year with family in other cities or in the countryside.

After thirty minutes, the car slowed. Mrs Vo had grown nervous as they penetrated the poorest parts of the city with no sign of anyone she might turn to for help if she needed it.

'There.' The driver pointed down a dark, filthy alley.

A faint recollection gathered at the back of Mrs Vo's mind, but it was indistinct, playing tricks with shadows and perspectives as she tried to make the street come into her memory more clearly. Not detailed enough. She didn't trust it. Didn't trust her memories. She was being fooled by her desire that this was the place. The way forward peered at her with unseen eyes, whispered with unheard words, threatened with menacing fear.

The driver was demanding a sum of money. It seemed excessive, but she wanted to be out of the cab, to take in where she was. She fumbled in her purse, her mind racing. I am a single woman in this out-of-the-way place. With a handbag full of money and no sign of anyone to protect me against mugging. Why did I bring all this money? She knew why. But what if this was the wrong place? If I dismiss the taxi, how will I get back to the hotel? An edge of panic rose in the pit of her stomach.

She handed the driver some notes. 'You wait here,' she commanded. 'I'll look for what I am after. If I don't return in ten minutes, then you can go. Okay?'

The driver eyed her suspiciously. 'What are you after?'

She turned and walked into the alley. 'Wait here!' she called over her shoulder.

But even before she had finished the order, she heard the taxi driving off. 'Fukka barfard!' She waited in the silence. Somewhere, water started running, a voice shouted, a door banged shut then even deeper silence. She took three steps further into the alley. The foul-smelling walls closed in on her as her eyes searched for something to recognise, anything from that time. But there was nothing. She was becoming trapped in fear emerging out of the grimy walls, deep-seated fear from long ago. The sound of shots being fired, screams and running feet came back to her. She closed her eyes, waiting for the door to be pushed open, for the rough hands to drag her outside, the feel of a cold metal gun barrel pushing against her temple.

She leapt back as something cold brushed her hand. Her hand went to her face while the other clutched the handbag close to her chest. A child was beside her, staring. A little girl, wide eyes inquiring. The little girl took her hand again and began to move off down the alley.

'Where are we going?' Mrs Vo managed to ask.

The little girl simply said, 'Grandfather'.

She hadn't seen the child approach, but that was the nature of this district. It was full of hidden byways, a maze of alleys and lanes, narrow thoroughfares that all led somewhere, but in which a stranger would become completely lost within seconds of entering. Now, for the first time that morning, she knew she was in the right place, the sense of it was what she remembered.

They hadn't gone far when the girl pointed at a pile of rotting wood leaning up against a wall of some sort. Rubbish rotted around the pile and two large black rats scurried away as the two of them approached.

The girl pointed at the woodpile. 'Grandfather,' she said. She gripped the woodpile and moved it to one side.

Mrs Vo was surprised to see that it was a gate of some kind. The girl motioned for her to walk into a dark space which had been revealed. Mrs Vo obeyed with trepidation. The girl pulled back a hessian hanging and Duong Vo had to adjust her eyes.

Before her was a courtyard filled with sunlight and flowers. A small ornamental pond with three goldfish was sitting amidst a bed of yellow and russet mini marigolds. There were dark-leaved cumquats in pots with orange fruits hanging on the branches. A culvert channelled clear running water which trickled into the pond. Where that come from?

she marvelled. In the far corner, she saw an exquisitely fashioned shrine with incense burning before a small golden Buddha. This is a nunnery she thought, looking around for the child.

The scale of the courtyard was so small that Mrs Vo was able to take in much of it at a glance. Its beauty awed her but she was struggling to recognise this as the place where she and Nga had been hidden in those terrible days after the fall of Saigon. The two cadres had been captured by South Vietnamese soldiers on the outskirts of Saigon days before it finally fell. They had been dragged into a house, raped repeatedly, beaten senseless and left for dead in the ruins of that suburb. When the North Vietnamese cadres entered the house, both women pretended to be dead, lying outstretched in their blood, vomit and muck. The cadres hadn't even checked their bodies so the rudimentary deception worked and they were left to rot along with the other detritus. Neither of them was in a state to get up and flee. Nga had intense pain in her pelvis and Duong Vo suspected it had been fractured. Her own hip was excruciating and her shoulder ached, but she refused to think about it. 'It'll be all right, all right,' she repeated over and over, a mantra to bypass the pain.

How many days they lie there, bombs falling nearby, the bursts of gunfire, shouts coming from both sides? It can't have been more than a day or two before the district fell silent. The sounds of war had moved on and Duong Vo realised that it was all happening closer to the city centre. The Viet Cong were capturing Saigon. They were her people in this fight. Then the sounds of helicopters drowned out everything and then it stopped. The world was silent, choking in the smell of cordite, rotting bodies and burning wood. Victory!

She woke. Scuffling sounds nearby. Terror gripped her heart. Big river rats were coming to tear the flesh off their bodies, eat them alive. A small cry escaped her and the scuffling stopped.

'Here.' A woman's voice!

Fingers feeling her body, pressing gently, then depressing her hip. Fiery shards of pain searing her body. Blackness descended as small hands lifted her onto a hard wooden pallet. She was aware they were moving. They were entering the burnt-out remains of a huge stone building. A body was hanging over the remains of the doorway, arms outstretched, feet clamped together on a cross. She knew that image. Jesus Christ. She was being taken into a Catholic church. The solace of the Southerners, the opiate of the masses. Their God had abandoned them. Then she blacked out again.

'Don't move.' A thin young man was stooped over her. His face had been smashed in on one side, skewing his jawline, flattening his nose and collapsing the eye socket so that only a hint of white showed through the bruised slit. It was a terrifying face, a face from stories her grandmother used to tell about demons on the mountains surrounding Hanoi. By contrast, the voice out of that crushed mouth was a flow of mumbled reassurances and soothing gentleness. 'You have to rest.'

She lifted her head to look around. This was not a church. They were in a very small space littered with metal shrapnel, which formed what looked like barricades.

'Shelters,' he said following her look. 'For when it rains.'

A burst of gunfire sounded so close it might have been in the compound. The young man disappeared, pulling down flaps of beaten shrapnel, covering Duong Vo, hiding her from sight. She cowered as the sounds of running feet passed by her head, something banging on the metal covers as they passed. Batons striking flesh. Demands to be answered. The voices hysterical with hatred. She heard the young man pleading, his voice breaking. Commands shouted. 'Kneel.' Knees cracking against stone. Shrieks of terror. A single gunshot. Silence! Feet marching away. Quiet sobbing threading around the beaten shrapnel.

Duong Vo wondered if she was the one crying. But her mind blanked out to the quiet lamentations of women's voices. Two days later, the marching feet returned. She heard metal flaps being dragged aside. Her flap was torn open but she was missed, so emaciated she had disappeared into the shadows of the shelter. Nga's screams, denying desertion. Nga's here! Duong Vo wanted to call her name. A single gunshot. This time, only Duong Vo was quietly sobbing.

'We have to get rid of them or we'll all be killed.' A man's voice. 'Too many informers.' A short silence. 'Yes, Father. I'll find a boat.'

'…have to get rid of them.' Mrs Vo blinked away memories. It's been forty years. Have you been there all the time? Or has this placed reawakened you from the deep sleep of forgetfulness? The memories were so vivid that the force of them had caught her off guard. Refocus! Of course you remembered. Always remembered. You came here to find out who saved your life. This is the place where Nga died. That unfortunate young man died. But I survived. Why me? Why not the others?

The dark past became suffused with the sunlit courtyard. The bungalow to the right looked makeshift, and small. A very old man was sitting on the stairs, looking straight ahead. The little girl was beside him, a small hand pressing his shoulder.

'Welcome,' he said. 'Happy New Year.'

After all this time, Duong Vo recognised the unmistakable voice. 'Happy New Year, Father.'

He smiled. 'Not Father any more,' and he gestured towards the shrine. 'The war changed many things.' He didn't stop looking ahead, which was disconcerting.

Mrs Vo took a step towards him and only then, when she was closer, did she realise that he was blind, the eyes opaque in the sunken sockets. 'Yes,' she said, 'now I see.'

He chuckled, nodding into that inward place where he had gathered his knowledge of the world. 'I was very happy to get your letter.'

My letter! How did it get to this place? Taking a long shot, she had addressed it to the Catholic church where they had been taken first all those years ago. Wanted to know who had read it to him. The little girl was too young. Was she, though? She looked around at the bright flowers in the garden, the pond with its fountain and goldfish. The compound was an oasis in the midst of poverty and dwellings decaying in the tropical heat and damp. Who looks after this?

Of course, he wouldn't know what it was like outside the narrow confines of these walls. This is his world. She now took a closer look at him, studying him, knowing he could not see her watching him. He was simply dressed in the Vietnamese manner – loose black pants and a white shirt. Both were spotlessly clean. How does he manage this cleanliness? His feet were covered with a pair of worn sandals exposing gnarled, knotted toes. He must be crippled, she thought. Rheumatism?

'Tuc, bring us tea, please.'

The little girl disappeared inside the shack.

'Why have you come?'

'I want to understand why I was saved, why only me?'

The old priest was nodding. 'Yes, why me?'

There was a long silence. Has he forgotten the question? Is he still attending to me? Those eyes give away nothing. She wanted to sit down on the stool under the shade of the fragrant frangipani tree in the corner, but didn't want to be presumptuous. Her body made a slight inclination towards it.

The old priest roused himself. 'My apologies. I should have invited you to sit down when you arrived. Please take the stool. It is cooling under the tree.'

Her surprise escaped in a sudden intake of breath.

'Ah,' he smiled, 'we compensate for what we lose. Please sit.'

Mrs Vo sat down and sipped the sweet ginger tea that Tuc had brought into the courtyard.

'Those were terrible days when the city fell. When the nuns found you and your friend, you were in a very bad way. Those soldiers had been very brutal. We did not think you would survive. The Mother Superior put two nuns in charge of you and the other girl. To see if they could nurse you back to health. They prayed, held vigils and gave what treatment they could. It was very little. No medicines, no ointments. They used traditional methods, but you should have been in hospital. There was no hospital, of course, and you wouldn't have been safe there. Somehow, by the will of God, the two of you began to recover. But then the betrayals started. There was one person in our community who traded with the Viet Cong. Gave information for small food par-

cels, things like that. Bartering his immortal soul for what? Protection?'
He let out a sad sigh and fell silent again.

Bees in the garden hummed, early morning heat opened blossoms.
Tiny insects poised in anticipation.

'Go on. Tell. I need to know, to understand.' Mrs Vo took a long
sip of the ginger tea, soothing herself.

'At first we did not know how the soldiers knew where to look. You
and your friend were not the only ones we were hiding, but one by one,
the others were taken. We kept moving them around, but the soldiers
always knew where to find them. Many were shot in front of us. All
I could do was administer the last rites, even though I had no idea if
they were Catholics. I had no oil, no vestments. Just holy water. They
took Dr Phong. You will remember Phong. He was disfigured from
a previous encounter with soldiers. Then your friend was taken. We
knew we had to do something. We decided to move you and others to
a different place. Nowhere was safe. The convent had become a trap.
We made preparations, but when the time came to move out, a small
group of soldiers appeared. They rounded us up and started shooting.
The nuns were killed first, then the others we had been hiding.'

Mrs Vo was rigid, holding in her emotions. 'How did I escape?'
What happened to his eyes? How did he escape? She closed her hands
around the cup and drained the tea too quickly. The refreshing sweet-
ness caught in her throat. She coughed and Tuc ran to her and patted
her back. She smiled and motioned to the girl that she was all right. 'I
can't remember what happened. How did I get out?'

The old priest sucked in his toothless gums, recalling those days of
disorder and butchery. 'I had set up a makeshift altar on your shrapnel
shelter. There was one flat piece of metal I used for the tabernacle and
chalice. I was conducting a final mass before we departed. The soldiers
were ruthless from the moment they came in. I was shoved face down
on the altar. My arms were spread across the shrapnel while they threw
large chunks of metal onto my hands, smashing them down. They hit
my feet with metal bars, splitting the skin, breaking bones.'

Mrs Vo tried to recall any of this, but her mind was closed against it. Her eyes were riveted on the old man as he recounted the horror of that morning. He drew his hands out of the long sleeves and held them up. She hadn't questioned why his hands were concealed, but now when she looked at them, she saw they were as broken and gnarled as his feet. She covered her face with her hands, wanted to run from the compound, wanted to unhear what she had already heard. Wanted not to hear the rest. But she stayed, compelled to grasp some detail of this reality and match it with her own while thanking God she could recall none of it.

'A soldier, a boy really, held a gun to my head. Soldiers were hammering on the shards, chanting slogans. I was acutely aware of the boy trembling, jerking the gun against my head. They raped the nuns one at a time then shot them. The bodies were piling up like shrapnel, one on top of the other. To my everlasting shame, I wasn't able to pray for them through the pain and terror inside me.' He paused, a single tear trickling from those inwardly seeing eyes. 'Then it was my turn. They came to drag me away from the altar. But as they did, there was a burst of flame that spread over the piles of metal. I had only one instant to see that flames were bursting out all around the piles, small but deadly explosions that seared my eyes, burnt hair, skin, clothes. And in the middle of the courtyard Mother Superior stood, an apparition of the Archangel Uriel, the other face of God, the light of God. The last thing I ever saw was her habit catching on fire, surrounded by burning soldiers screaming into a glorious Communist eternity. I lost my sight and consciousness to the sounds of Mother Superior's agonised screams as she burnt...'

They sat in silence for a long time, the old man reliving that day, Mrs Vo struggling to understand how she was going to live the rest of her life with those images. Would it have been better never to have known?

The old priest was speaking again and she roused herself to listen.

'To this day I don't know what happened. I can only assume that there were pockets of unexploded flammable substances that we had been surrounded by all the time. Phosphorus, gunpowder? The metal scraping across metal must have set up sparks which ignited that substance.'

Duong Vo's voice was quavering. 'We survived?'

'You were under the altar and miraculously didn't get burnt. People came to put out the fires to stop them spreading through the neighbourhood. They found us. Some of them were from my Catholic congregation and took me in. When I regained consciousness, I told them to put you on that boat we had paid for. That's what they did and you ended up in Australia. I am very happy for you.'

They sat in silence for some time, as the garden hummed around them and the sun slowly etched shadows across the tubs of golden marigolds and stacked them up the far wall of the courtyard. A cough roused Duong Vo. Tuc was standing in the doorway to the bungalow, looking intently at her. Duong Vo smiled at the girl. Yes, it's time to go she thought.

A mosquito zizzed down her arm and landed on her hand. She raised the other hand to swipe it, but was taken aback by the look that came into Tuc's eyes. Oh God! This is a Buddhist society. I'm in a Buddhist household. All life is sacred. She flicked her hand and the mosquito flew off, but not before it had had a taste of her blood.

Land of blood, she sighed. My poor Vietnam. The Tet offensive had been a bloodbath, an ominous prelude to the end of the war. And yet they survived the cataclysm, she thought, looking from Tuc to the priest. He saved me. What does it mean?

She took from her handbag the envelope of banknotes and stepped forward. In a gesture of obeisance, she bowed deeply before the priest with her hands holding the cash out in front of her.

The priest tilted his head to hear what was happening, but now there was only the sound of birds and insects. He stretched a hand to Tuc, who came and stood beside him, whispering quietly. A benign look spread across his face. Duong Vo could see, even from this position, that he was nodding.

Then he stood up and reached out to her. He straightened her to face him. 'You owe me nothing,' he said solemnly.

'To help with your life,' Duong Vo whispered.

'There are many more in need in this country than me. Thank you, but I cannot take your offering.' He smiled in Tuc's direction. 'I have everything I need here.'

Back in her hotel room that afternoon, Duong Vo thought about what the priest had told her. Flashes of those days had come to her as she was driven back in the car the priest had managed to get for her. Not a taxi, but a private car driven by a young woman who said nothing about herself or her connection to the priest, but would talk only about the Tet holiday.

Duong Vo had always had trouble picturing Nga and their flight together. The day the church was raided and the nuns murdered had lived in her memory as a phantasm of screams and desperate shouts, the smell of burning flesh, explosions like firecrackers and hammering. She would never be clear about her rescue from that place and getting onto the boat out of Vietnam. But now she knew how it ended in Saigon. If that was all it was to be, then she accepted it.

The priest is happy for me in Australia. Am I happy for me? Duong pondered this question for a long time. Yes, I'm alive. I'm happy. Australia is good.

Duong Vo did a lot of research into not-for-profit organisations providing for girls in need and distress in Ho Chi Minh City. She donated a large gift of money to an organisation she liked and got a flurry of thank yous, pamphlets about the work they do and many pictures of the girls they help. She cleared a space on the chest in her lounge room and arranged them there so she could look at them.

'My Vietnam' she would say. 'My Vietnam, my Australia.'

Old Grizzlepuss

'I don't want to! Mummy, I don't want to!'

The child's whine rang through the house. It was impossible to ignore. The urgent, hushed attempts by his mother to short-circuit the protests only made them grow louder.

Staring out the window at the garden, Charles William squared his shoulders against his grandson's rebuff. Pursing his lips, he straightened his back in defiance.

'Why do I have to go to the park? Grandad doesn't like it. Why can't he take Bella?'

Manipulative little bugger, Charles William thought, and wondered why he was ever nice to his only grandson. It was difficult often enough, being civil to the parents, without putting up with the child's lack of discipline and that penetrating shrill voice.

He'd told Catherine, his wife, that morning, before the family arrived, that Sunday lunch was a family institution he could well do without.

'But Charles, when would we ever see them?'

Her dismay had been mildly pleasing to him, a small wounding without real hurt. But then she had gone on to spoil his sense of satisfaction.

'Anthony is just going through a difficult phase. He'll get over it. Children are like that. He's a delight, really.'

She sounded so sure of herself that he didn't know how to reply. Catherine had always been able to counter him with unanswerable explanations. A quality he both admired and disliked in her. Well, if Sunday lunches are to continue, then he'd be damned if excursions to the park have to be a part of it. However, Catherine had tutted and organised the luncheon with enough time for him to take Anthony to the park.

Now, he was feeling really irritated with the whole lot of them. With lunch sitting heavily on his stomach, his own fault for overeating, he stared out the window at the bank of white azaleas, wanting it to be over. 'I think I shall go and read in my study,' he announced.

Catherine came to his side holding his jacket, looking into his face. 'Now, Charles, you're not to carry on. Please. Elizabeth is just getting his parka on. You don't have to stay long if it's too cold, but the boy does need to wear off some of that energy. We don't want him tearing around the house knocking things over. We've been through this. You always take him to the park after lunch on Sunday. It's time you have together. He expects it. We all do. Besides, you like it. You know you do. All those rich old fogies and their money talk. Why don't you ask Michael to go along with you?'

'Michael! I've just sat through lunch listening to his half-cocked drivel about things he has no understanding of. If I have to go to the park with his ungrateful son, I'd rather go without Michael.'

'Charles!'

The outburst left them both not knowing what to say. Charles William turned and made his way to the hall, leaving Catherine at the window. She worried as to what had brought this on. It was another cause for concern in what seemed to be a developing pattern of erratic and unpredictable behaviour from her husband.

Charles William had always been a bit irascible. Is today's behaviour more of the same? Why is he resenting taking Anthony to the park? That's what grandfathers do. And now he doesn't want Michael to accompany them.

In the past there had been bouts of restrained contempt in the lunchtime arguments between Charles and Michael, but today they had kept a lid on the antagonism. That is, until Charles's comments a moment ago. Michael had been rather more sententious than usual at lunch, but on the whole she thought the meal had flowed rather smoothly, considering the men's dislike of each other.

In the hall, Elizabeth bit her bottom lip as Anthony made three clumsy attempts before successfully zipping up his parka. It was an ordinary thing for a little boy to learn, but her father stood waiting impatiently at the door, eyes fixed on the moulded plasterwork on the ceiling. Michael was lolling in the dining room doorway, uttering a droning monologue about the value of the Aussie dollar against the greenback.

'I want to go on the swings, the seesaw…'

'And the slippery slide,' Michael added now that his son seemed to have changed his mind about the park.

'No, Daddy.'

'He's frightened of the slippery slide,' Elizabeth whispered.

'I think you should let Grandad take you on that.'

'No! Not the slippery slide. Mummy!' Anthony wailed.

'Michael, please! No, darling. You don't have to if you don't want to.' Elizabeth knelt down and retied one of her son's shoelaces.

'Why not?' Michael's tone was goading. 'There's nothing to be frightened of. What are you frightened of, Anthony?'

'Mike, please!'

'I don't want to, Mummy. I don't have to, do I?'

'For heaven's sake, Mike. Leave him alone. No, Anthony, you don't have to do anything you don't want to do. Grandad will be with you. You two can have fun.'

Anthony looked suspiciously at his grandfather. Charles William wished he had been more attentive at lunch to Michael's talk about currencies. An alarming thought was forming in his mind about Michael's intentions. However, his concentration wavered when his son-in-law was concerned. Despite spending his own lifetime organising other people's finances, he couldn't stand the way Michael was such a know-all about organising the world for everybody else. I don't need your advice, he grumbled to himself.

But then, he didn't feel like defending Anthony either, and the boy was scowling at him.

'I can't see what all the fuss is about,' Michael persisted, oblivious to the silence that had descended in the hall. 'Grandad will be with you. You don't think he'd let anything happen to you, do you?'

The little boy clutched at his mother's skirt, tears standing in the corners of his eyes. 'I don't want to go, Mummy. I don't want to go to the park,' he whispered.

Michael had crouched down, on the point of doing some very straight talking to his son when Charles William suddenly leant across and poked him in the chest with his walking stick. Michael pulled back in surprise.

'I know what you're up to. Don't think I don't. Well, you won't get away with it. What's mine is mine and I'll do with it as I wish. You invest how you please, but leave my money to me. Come on, sonny, are we going to the park or not?' Charles William took Anthony by the hand and opened the door.

'I don't want to go with you. You hit my daddy.'

'We always go to the park on Sunday.' Charles William felt very pleased with himself and in complete control. 'Don't be a grizzlepuss. Come on.'

'Grizzlepuss? That's funny. You're a grizzlepuss. An old grizzlepuss.'

'Anthony!' Elizabeth raised her finger in warning to her son.

'And you're a double old grizzlepuss!' Charles William egged his grandson on.

'And you're a…

The child's giggles receded as Charles William marched them both out the door, closing it firmly on his family.

Elizabeth's eyes flickered from her husband to her mother, trying to assess the situation. Catherine had not recovered from Charles William's outburst in the lounge room and was now distressed and bewildered at what had just happened.

'What's got into him?' Michael was seething. He had been humiliated in front of his wife, his son and his mother-in-law. He was desperately searching for some words that would denigrate Charles William and cover his own overwhelming sense of impotence at what had happened. 'I mean to say, you don't exactly expect to be assaulted by your father-in-law with a walking stick at Sunday lunch!'

Michael could hear how foolish he sounded. He'd drunk too much wine to deliver a real demolition job on Charles William. Then there was the stinging image of the old man poking him with the stick: long arms extended, one leg forward, the stick thrust at his chest like a foil. It was almost absurdly funny if it hadn't been so bloody stupid and demeaning.

It flashed through Catherine's head that perhaps most men were bullies underneath it all, but that you never saw it till the surface began to crack. Maybe Charles William was cracking. Maybe she was.

'Dad's never behaved like that before, Mike.' Elizabeth blundered between her torn loyalties. 'He didn't mean to poke you with the stick. I think you upset him at lunch.'

Mike started to protest.

'Well, you did go on about the financial thing. You know how secretive he is about all that. And you shouldn't go on at Anthony, either. He is only four.'

'Oh, of course it would be my fault, wouldn't it?'

Catherine turned and walked upstairs. I really don't want to hear them argue. She closed her bedroom door and stretched out on the chaise longue. She ran her hand along the silken brocade, calming herself with its reassuring quality. She and Charles had purchased the chaise when they first became engaged. It had been so dilapidated and quite a bargain. Searching for the fabric had been such fun and then finding an upholsterer who would mend the frame, add firmer padding and cover it with the brocade. She closed her eyes, remembering the two of them rambling through Sunday afternoons in antique shops and second-hand furniture stores. They had turned many a head as they strolled along, arm in arm.

Is he becoming more erratic? Or am I just noticing it for the first time? It might be a consequence of his retirement, of course, although he still has his consultancy work with the firm. He seems to enjoy that.

Gets him out of the house. Come to think of it, though, he does seem more obsessed with money these days. And what was all that about Michael being up to something? Michael had been doing an awful lot of prying into their finances and Charles William had clearly been getting more and more exasperated by it

Perhaps he is right about Sunday lunches. But I can't abandon them! It's what we do. None of this tension really makes any sense. Something is amiss. The more I think about it… Tsk! I'll just have to have it out with him tonight. The sooner I get to the bottom of what is bothering him, the sooner something can be done about it.

Catherine had drifted off. She awoke, disoriented by a commotion downstairs. Anthony's squeaky voice was piping out some story to his parents. Good God, what is it now?

Descending the stairs she was greeted by Elizabeth, Michael and Anthony's upturned faces. Silence – commotion and silence. It was all too unnerving. In the guest room, Bella woke and started cooing for her mother. The soft baby sounds emphasised the stillness in the hall.

'Where's Charles?' Catherine worked to keep her panic at bay. 'Where is he? What's happened?' Her voice was strained and quavering.

'He's all right, Mum. Nothing's happened. Well, nothing serious.'

'What is it?' Catherine crossed to her daughter. 'Tell me.'

'He's not hurt. Really, he's all right. Anthony says he did something.'

Anthony was bobbing up and down beside his mother in a state of high excitement. Bella was yelling now and Elizabeth moved towards the stairs.

Anthony couldn't contain himself a moment longer and blurted out, 'Grandad did wee-wee. In front of the swings and everyone saw him and a man told him to stop but he didn't and we all saw his thing hanging out with the wee coming.'

'Anthony!'

'Whoosh, whoosh. It went everywhere.'

'Anthony! For God's sake, Mike, take him out.'

'He did, he did. It's true. Everybody saw him.'

Michael steered the boy out of the room on a tide of the child's protests.

Bella's cries had risen to shrieks and Elizabeth ran up the stairs.

'I'll get her. Don't worry, Mum. It's probably nothing like that. You know what kids are like.' She hurried past her mother, her own mind in turmoil as to what might have happened in the park.

Catherine stood frozen. Indeed, I do know what kids are like, she reasoned. Anthony might be a bit trying at times but he did not tell lies. She sat down on the stairs facing the front door. Her heart was beating too quickly and she struggled for breath. Is it a brain tumour? Oh dear God, don't let this happen, please, please. Not to us. The only thing that has ever really mattered to him is his mind. If he loses that...?

Charles William walked in flushed from exercise and the cold. It struck him immediately as odd that his wife was sitting on the stairs looking at him.

'Hello. The boy get in all right?'

Catherine just stared at him.

'What are you doing there, old thing?'

She felt a nerve in her cheek flickering. Is it some kind of joke? How do I ask my husband of forty-five years if he urinated in front of everybody at the park?

'Charles, are you all right?'

'Of course I'm all right. Why wouldn't I be?' Everyone really was being very peculiar this afternoon.

Elizabeth peered down from the landing with Bella in her arms. Her father seemed so matter-of-fact. It couldn't have happened. Not the way Anthony told it.

'Did you have a nice time, Dad?'

'Yes, I had a nice time. What's got into you two?'

The women staring as if they were seeing a ghost was unnerving. He raised his voice to reassert control. 'Catherine?'

Then Michael was roaring from the back of the house. 'Anthony! Anthony! Come back here. Anthony!'

The little boy careered into the hall with a mischievous grin on his face. 'Did you tell them Grandad? Did you?'

Michael rushed in and angrily grabbed his son. 'Didn't I tell you not to come in here?' He gave his son a sharp slap on the leg and Anthony screamed, trying to pull away.

'Tell them what?'

'Anthony, that's enough.' Elizabeth motioned to Michael to take him away.

With a look of contempt at Charles William, he dragged the screaming child out of the hall and closed the door.

Catherine couldn't bear the look on Charles William's face. 'Charles, did anything happen in the park?'

'What is this all about, Cat? Will someone give me a straight answer, please?'

Bella was nuzzling at her mother's breast, beginning to fret. Poor little mite, she must be starving. Elizabeth unbuttoned her blouse.

'Dad, Anthony said you urinated in the park.' She knew her mother could never say it.

'The devil he did. Little bugger.'

It was Charles William's look of wide-eyed amazement which convinced Catherine not only that he had done it, but that he knew he had.

'Charles, tell me truly. Did you do it?'

'You're not serious, old girl, are you?' He dropped his gaze and walked between the two women, upstairs to the bedroom, where they heard the door click shut.

Catherine made tea while Elizabeth sat in the sunroom feeding Bella. She could hear Michael grilling her grandson mercilessly about what had happened in the park. Her head was beginning to ache and she closed her eyes as Anthony's story increasingly became unravelled under his father's aggressive interrogation.

'Michael, he's only four,' Elizabeth whispered to herself. 'He's still a baby.'

When Catherine brought in the tea, none of them said anything about the park. Not even when she took a cup upstairs to Charles William.

The next few weeks were hell for Catherine. She had to apologise to young Dirk Hansen, who had been really decent when he came and told her about 'the incident'. She watched as neighbours skulked behind bushes to avoid speaking to Charles William as he passed.

Over the next two years, Charles William increasingly forgot things, missed appointments and became more and more muddled. Catherine silenced her terror by devising more and more complicated ruses to cover for him. She looked for signs of physical decay, a swelling, headaches, loss of appetite, but saw none. Most days, she would dial at least one physician's number, but always hung up when the receptionist answered.

The situation with Charles William came to a head the day he went out for a walk in the park and didn't come back. By late afternoon, Catherine was in a panic and phoned the local police station. When a patrol car pulled up outside the house sometime later with Charles William in the back seat, calmly waving to her out the window, Catherine went through an emotional turmoil of anger and relief.

The police told her they had found Charles William sitting on a seat at a bus stop on the main road. He told the police he was watching the people coming home from work.

After she had thanked the police, she berated Charles William for getting lost.

'I wasn't lost,' he protested. 'I went for a walk. You're always telling me I need more exercise. You're just a silly old fusspot. You don't need to worry about me.'

A week later, Charles William went for a walk and disappeared again for a few hours. Catherine got into the car and drove around looking for him. She found him sitting on a wall outside a church, just sitting there watching the birds swooping down to feed then flying back up into the trees. The disappearances developed into a pattern that left Catherine frustrated and in a quandary. She was afraid he might be hit by a car crossing the road or that he might actually forget the way home. She wondered if he hadn't already forgotten where he lived.

Unable to bear the sole responsibility for Charles William any longer, she rang and invited Elizabeth to lunch. She would enlist her daughter's assistance in coming to terms with her husband's worrying behaviour. Elizabeth arrived, kids in tow. Somehow, Catherine had not expected this and felt very put out by the children being there. The salmon mousse reminded Elizabeth of the Sunday lunch, the lunch when Anthony told his story about his grandfather weeing in the park. Please don't let him have done something like that again, Elizabeth prayed.

Catherine was on the verge of bringing up her concerns when Elizabeth said, 'You know, Mum, I hope you don't mind me saying this, but you were supposed to meet me at Café Rouge last Wednesday. We were going to go shopping for the kids, remember? I rang and rang, but you didn't answer. I was worried sick.'

Catherine pushed mousse around her plate trying to remember the arrangement, trying to remember what she had been doing last Wednesday. 'I'm sorry, darling. Are you sure? Let me check…'

'Mum, don't think me rude, but I looked in your diary. It's there. Look, I guess what I'm suggesting is that you ought to have a check-up. Don't get upset. It's just that you've been looking a little run-down, that's all. You might need a vitamin shot or something. You've lost weight too. Are you dieting?'

Catherine sat looking at her plate, desperately trying to remember what she had done last Wednesday. She couldn't remember what she had done on any of the days last week. She felt utterly trapped in a web of her own deceptions and anxiety about Charles William. About herself. Here were her beautiful daughter and grandchildren and she was going to lose them all. She couldn't bear it and quite suddenly she was crying. It was she who was cracking, crying in front of Elizabeth and the children.

'Why is Granny crying, Mummy?' Anthony whispered.

'Why don't you go outside and play, darling?'

'I haven't finished my pie and tomato sauce.'

'Anthony, please do as Mummy says. Take the pie outside and when you finish it you can play.'

'No.'

Elizabeth skirted around her frustration and went to hug her mother. 'What is it, Mum? You're not telling me things and it's really odd. There is something, isn't there? Have you seen Doctor McFadden?'

'Is Granny sick?'

Catherine shook her head and tried to smile at the boy. There was no way she could tell Elizabeth like this. She shouldn't have invited her. How could she have forgotten the children would also be coming? That's why I bought the pie, and anyway, Bella is still breastfeeding. It was stupid.

'I'm all right really. Just a bit fraught. I'm sorry, darling. Eat your pie. I'll give you a ring tonight. Granny's just being an old silly, my boy chick.'

'Boy chick. I'm not a chick,' Anthony giggled.

'We're out tonight, Mum. Look, why don't I phone McFadden now and make an appointment for you? I can call you tomorrow and see how you are.'

'No. I'm all right, really. Your question threw me, that's all. Let me clear these things away and I'll get cheese.'

'And ice cream for me, Granny.' Anthony stared at her with big eyes. He had never seen Granny cry before and he didn't like it.

That evening Charles William was late again. Catherine was rung by security at the office where he had established his firm some thirty years ago. They told her he had gone to the toilet in one of the pot plants in the foyer of the building. He had insisted that it was a urinal. The guard told her Charles was confused and a bit stroppy, but that they had calmed him and put him in a cab. He should be arriving home in about fifteen minutes.

And so here we are, she told herself. We've reached the end of our time together in this lovely house.

Casting her eyes around the living room, she couldn't help admiring the upholstered sofas, the small side tables and the standard lamps. They were showing signs of age and wear, but were still in good condition. At the same time she began appraising the value of the furniture, ornaments, paintings and rugs. Nobody wants this old style any more, she thought, reflecting on the assessment an antique dealer from Mosman had given her some months ago. No resale value, only value to me. I shall miss it all.

She had been going over and over in her mind the odd incidents of Charles's behaviour and of her own growing uncertainty about her ability to cope with him. Finally, after consulting Dr McFadden and discussing the situation with Elizabeth and Michael, she resolved that Charles William really had to go into residential care.

She rang Dr McFadden's surgery. Diane put her straight through and he outlined a series of tests he wanted Charles William to take. The diagnosis of dementia after weeks of brain scans, blood tests and discussions in the doctor's rooms was almost a relief for Catherine. At least it wasn't cancer, she thought, but worse in some ways. It was the end for Charles William, although he would never really know it. She couldn't bear the thought of him reduced to a vegetable state.

One morning, she found herself wishing it had been cancer and that he could go quickly. The fact that she had even thought it distressed her for days afterwards.

'Mum, let me do the research on nursing homes,' Elizabeth said after Catherine had told her the diagnosis.

Catherine felt an immense sense of relief. A surge of love for her daughter swept over her. She surprised Elizabeth by giving her a hug, something which was rather uncharacteristic in their relationship.

They settled Charles William into The Gables at Northstar Residential Care.

'What is this place?' Charles William asked when Elizabeth and Catherine showed him the small apartment where he was to spend the rest of his life.

'It's like a holiday resort, Dad,' Elizabeth replied without hesitation.

'Then after the holiday, I'll go home,' Charles William confided to the carer who was showing them around.

After she and Elizabeth had settled Charles William into his new accommodation, Catherine went home, where she was suddenly alone with the chasm that had opened between her and the rest of the world. She had never felt so lonely and isolated, despite almost daily visits to The Gables, friends rallying and Elizabeth's unflagging attentions.

It seemed that she would eventually have to sell the house and find an apartment closer to Elizabeth and the kids. But she was determined to stay in the house for as long as she could manage.

'No, darling,' Catherine protested to Elizabeth, 'of course I can manage. I'll bump Heidi the cleaner up two days a week. Bob can keep doing the garden and I can alternate between cooking and ordering in meals. There are some really fine dining services.'

But Elizabeth and Michael were insistent and put the house on the market. Elizabeth took her mother out when estate agents came round or brought potential purchasers to inspect the property.

'It's not property,' Catherine mouthed at Elizabeth's retreating car after the 'For Sale' sign went up at the front. 'It's my home. Our family home, Charles's and mine.'

She wandered through the house touching and rearranging the beautiful things that she and Charles William had acquired during their marriage. 'How I will miss you,' she said out loud.

The rooms had already somehow changed, looking less homely, seeming a little…a little sad.

In the garden, she brushed the back of her hand against the last of the white azalea blossoms, so elegant against the dark green of the foliage. She walked along the path to the end of the garden and looked back at the house. It was beautiful in its spring mantle of crepuscule and albertine, climbing up from the border of sweet box. She breathed the perfumes of roses, lavender and jasmine. Perfection!

How odd to think that it will be here after we are gone. Who will look after it? What if a developer buys it?

She gave the house and garden a last look as Catherine, the owner. 'Property,' she murmured. 'Property!'

Then she turned and went back into the house, closing the back door behind her.

Through a Temple Gate

Lyle stopped abruptly at the circular temple gate. Goosebumps prickled across his skin as his heart began to beat faster. At the end of the path was a lion and it was staring at him. He knew he wouldn't be able to run, even if he wanted to. The lion was always going to be there. It would always be able to outrun him, grapple him to the ground and maul him.

Lyle murmured a prayer though it was inaudible in the silence.

Into the warm sunshine and gentle breeze of early morning, a jungle slowly grew around the lion. Lush vines gripped at massive tree trunks, hauling themselves upwards into the rich tangled greens of the canopy. Birds flew and darted from low branches to higher, monkeys swung from vine to vine like aerialists in some fantastic simian circus. And all the while blossoms, twigs, leaves and fruits tumbled through the humid air and landed among the undergrowth, softly thudding to the rhythm of his heart.

His ears rang with the long, whooping calls of birds with wide wingspans soaring overhead and the shrill trills of their smaller, brilliantly coloured avian cousins. Lyle tensed at the slithering, twisting movement of the leaf mould and litter on the forest floor. An ominous hiss rose from behind the temple wall. The serpent was coming. It would soon be here to get him. Every instinct in Lyle's body was urging him to flee.

A slight incline of his head attuned Lyle to more sounds: the constant drip, drip, drip of water deep in the jungle, its rhythmic percussion accompanying the hum and thrum of myriad insects hovering in the air, stretched across the gate like a silk screen painting in which the lion, poised to spring, was captured. It was as if Lyle was looking through a veil which those massive claws could rent apart at one blow.

Not a silk screen painting, Lyle told himself as his attention returned to the lion. It's a ceramic, a decoration. It sat atop a stone plinth, its green and red glazes accentuating the great bulging eyes fixed on him. The powerful claws were gripping the stone, keeping the lion stable. Or maybe it was sharpening its claws.

Lyle felt light-headed. He realised he had stopped breathing, and started gulping oxygen, filling his lungs as he drew in a big breath. He felt panicked and hugged himself to calm a tremble that was rippling around his body.

Then something extraordinary happened. The lion spoke to him.

'Don't be frightened.'

Lyle stopped breathing again.

'Keep breathing, Lyle.'

Lyle's eyes widened and he took in a deep breath. 'You're talking!' He blinked, but the lion was still there when he opened his eyes. 'How do you know my name?' he gasped.

'It's on the name tag.'

Lyle's hand flew to the name tag. He had forgotten the tag with his name and that of the hotel written in Chinese. In the distance, he thought he could hear voices, familiar voices, approaching from behind him.

'In this culture, I represent strength and stability,' the lion said. 'I am not a mere decoration.' The lion cocked his head and gave Lyle a chastening glance. 'I am here to guard this temple. That is the role the gods have assigned to me and I am proud to do it.'

'You look very strong,' Lyle ventured.

'The gods have made you strong too, Lyle.'

Lyle shook his head. 'No, I am weak, weak and hopeless.'

The lion shook his mane. 'Your spirit is strong. I feel it in this sacred place. Many people pass by me and I feel nothing. They snap a picture and move on to the temple, the main attraction. You are one of a select few who have stopped at the gate and come to understand some of the mystery of this place. That makes you special.'

The voices were getting louder, calling his name.

'Believe in your inner strength, Lyle. One day, you will be a man and people will look up to you. Remember this.'

A hand grabbed Lyle's shoulder roughly. 'How dare you go off like that,' his mother hissed.

'We've been looking everywhere for you, son.'

'It was irresponsible of you. What if something had happened to you? You're in a foreign country, no language to communicate, no sense of direction. What would you have done if you had got lost?'

'You are hopeless, son. Didn't it occur to you to come looking for us back at the pagoda?'

'There's no point bringing you overseas if you keep wandering off like this. We hoped you might learn a bit about other cultures, other people. Instead, you get lost and we find you standing here, gaping into space in some kind of daydream, not even going into the courtyard to look at the temple.'

'That's why we're here, to look at the temple.'

'If you can't keep up with us, Lyle, then we might have to leave you at the hotel while your father and I go sightseeing.'

His mother roughly pushed him between herself and his father. She gripped his hand and pulled him through the gate with her. 'Am I going to have to hold on to you the whole time we are away? Yes, don't shake your head. You are untrustworthy and that is a weakness in a boy.'

As they turned past the lion, the temple came fully into Lyle's view. It took his breath away. I would be strong if I had to guard this place, he thought and cast a last glance back over his shoulder at the lion.

'For God's sake, Lyle, look where you're going.'

The lion turned and nodded at Lyle. 'And I would be proud to have a strong and stable boy like you at my side,' it said.

Lyle knew that he was the only one who could hear it. He was the only one who had stopped and looked at the lion. He was the only one to conjure a jungle that day for the lion to stand in, not a savage jungle, a magical jungle of colour, movement and sounds. He locked the lion's words away in his heart, ready for the day when he would need them.

Delights and Disappointments

Christmas Eve. The usually cool interior of St Sebastian's had turned sultry as the thermometer climbed towards thirty degrees during the afternoon. Stuart Chapman was conducting, if you could call it that, the dress rehearsal for the Christmas pageant that the gay men and women of Saint Sebastian's were presenting before the midnight mass.

He turned to his assistant, Alison, and said, 'The temperature is going to be the least of my worries. Marshalling this unruly cast to run the dress rehearsal is like herding chickens in a barnyard.'

In front of the Lady Chapel, four women in overalls and boots were noisily removing pews in preparation for setting up the crib. They were ignoring Stuart's glares. The church organ was making a whirring sound of the kind that Alison knew might just make Stuart homicidal. The three wise men had hitched up their gowns to cool themselves. They were sprawled provocatively across some side pews, legs akimbo, talking and laughing. Stuart was snared between shock and titillation at catching a flash of underpants. Young Cameron was flapping the hem of his wise-man gown up and down to get some air circulating. Should I tell him? Stuart wondered, casting a second look at Cameron. He was distracted from the underpants by the emergence of two older women parishioners who began hassling the pew removalists to get on with it so they could clean the floor. The altercation was adding to the sense of chaos.

'Bloody butch dykes and dizzy queens,' Stuart fumed into the over-heated atmosphere.

Standing beside him, twisting her fingers in her anxiety, Alison mouthed the word 'charity', but left it unspoken, choosing to exercise forbearance over correction.

Stuart turned to her, exasperated. 'Where the bloody hell are the angels?' he demanded. 'I need the angels on stage now. And do you think it's too much to ask for the mother of the Son of God to be present at the birth? Do you think we could at least manage that?'

Alison felt aggrieved. She hated swearing at the best of times, but it was completely unacceptable in church. Besides, Stuart's tone to her was offensive. 'Bloody hell?' 'Barnyard?' We're talking about re-enacting the birth of the Saviour in a manger in a stable, not a barnyard. This time she felt compelled to correct him. 'It's not a stage, Stuart, it's a sanctuary.'

Stuart gritted his teeth. He was about to say something, but thought better of it when he saw the offended look on her face. I need her onside. He took out his handkerchief and mopped his brow. Dear God, can we have a bit of a breeze please, he prayed.

Alison had wavered in her attitude to Stuart ever since the pageant had been given approval by the bishop. He has campaigned long and hard to get the priest onside and make the church inclusive she thought, but he shouldn't let it go to his head. The rehearsals have been a nightmare! And now this shambles.

Stuart tucked his handkerchief back in his pocket with a grand flourish which was intended to demonstrate his mastery of the situation, but looked more like a retreat. He spoke calmly, or so he thought.

'Forgive me if I sound uncharitable, Alison,' he said, 'but I can't bloody direct and stage manage and do everything. I said I wanted the angels on stage after the run-through with the three wise men. So where are they?'

Alison shot an imploring look towards the vestry. What are they doing in there? she wondered. They've been in there for half an hour. It shouldn't take that long to slip on a robe and attach the wings to each other's backs. But the door to the vestry remained steadfastly shut. Should I go and see what the hold-up is?

'They're dressing,' she told him. 'The angel costumes have only just been delivered.'

'Ah, so the costumes have arrived in time for the dress rehearsal, have they? Bloody marvellous! His ladyship managed to pull his finger out and get on with it, did he?'

Alison decided she couldn't take any more of Stuart's swearing and attitude. As she started to move away, the vestry door opened and her son Martin came out followed by Jessica and Oliver. The angels were dressed in sleeveless, ankle-length, pleated pink gowns and had matching pink-feathered wings on their backs. A hush fell on the church for the first time since the dress rehearsal had begun. All eyes were fixed on the three young angels. The image they created as they stood there, wide-eyed and butter-wouldn't-melt-in-my-mouth picture perfect was pure Disney.

The silence was broken by a solitary voice from somewhere at the entrance of the church. 'Delightful! Three little Iced Vo Vos.'

'What!' Stuart expostulated. 'Who is that?' he asked into the silence that followed, but couldn't turn away from the beautiful angelic vision he had evoked with the choice of cast and the costumes.

All eyes other than the director's were now peering towards the church entrance, trying to see who the mystery speaker was.

'Well, they are gay angels,' Stuart snapped, half-turning towards the back to see who had spoken, while still reluctant to drag his eyes away from the vision before him.

Martin had been a favourite child of his in the parish. He liked Alison and had felt keenly for her when her husband, Martin's father, died four years ago. Martin had grown into a striking-looking young man, and with that Stuart's feelings had turned into something much more complex and disturbing. My special secret, he'd confided to himself.

Unobserved by Stuart, Alison fought back tears. This is my son, my only child standing in the sanctuary at Saint Sebastian's dressed in a long, pink flowing robe with two soft, feathered wings at his back. Dear Lord, how did this come to pass?

Stuart was transfixed at the way the robes fell in straight folds from the boys' tanned shoulders.

'More like Greek korai than Christian angels,' Alison whispered to Stuart. Her son Martin looked so handsome, as did his boyfriend, Oliver. And Jessica looked every bit the perfect Greek goddess, a Praxiteles in pink. Alison prayed silently, raising her eyes to the cross above the altar. 'Is this part of Your great design? Grant me the grace to accept what You have given me because I am finding it difficult.'

Even though Martin and Oliver had moved in together eight months ago, Alison still found it hard to accept that her son was gay. Not that she would ever let Martin know that she had difficulties over his sexuality. She didn't, really. Well, she ought not have, was more the truth. It's just that he had seemed such a heterosexual boy when he was growing up, and Oliver too, for that matter. All that sport. And the rowing team. There had been girlfriends and, if she was being honest with herself, compromising situations she had come across between Martin, Oliver and their girlfriends of the day. Perhaps the school's theatricals, which had meant so much to the boys, should have given her a clue as to what was to come, but it had all seemed so normal, just so much good fun.

Stuart made a massive effort to refocus, dragging his eyes away from Martin. He clapped his hands. 'All right, yes, very nice but don't just stand there. We haven't got all day to ogle you, you know. Get into your positions. Jessica, where's Megan, that girlfriend of yours? She was supposed to be here for the three wise men tableau. She is the Virgin Mary, after all.'

There were sniggers from the girls working on the crib. 'Virgin!' one of them snorted and the sniggers turned to mocking laughter.

A flush spread across Jessica's face. 'She's here, Stuart… somewhere.'

Stuart rolled his eyes and shook his head in an exaggerated gesture of despair. 'I can't produce a nativity play with the mother of the Son of God being "somewhere".' He flapped his hand at the angels. 'Centre stage, please. Wise men, here – you're in this scene too.'

'It's the sanctuary,' Alison whispered, and turned away to avoid Stuart's retort.

Stuart clenched his teeth in frustration and turned to Mathilde Kirschbaum, who was sitting straight-backed at the organ. She had been watching the proceedings with some amusement. Stuart nodded to her. Instantly, a massive chord erupted from the organ and progressed by thirds up two octaves. There was a cheer from the crib ladies which died down as Stuart took a menacing step towards the organist with a thunderous look on his face. The music stopped.

'Eine kleine Scherze, mein Gauleiter.' Mathilde turned and faced him. 'Ist lustig, nicht?'

'Nicht! Stuart growled. 'And you know I don't speak German.'

'Wirklich? Mein Gott!' Mathilde chuckled at the crib girls.

'It might be funny in deepest snowbound Prussia, Mathilde,' Stuart roared, 'which incidentally is not regarded as one of the centres of world comedy. But it's not funny in bloody thirty-degree heat in an Australian summer, with this shambolical rehearsal already half an hour behind schedule.'

There was a tutting from the entrance of the church.

Stuart glared at Alison. 'Can you get rid of whoever that is before I do something I will regret?'

Alison didn't move.

He turned back to Mathilde. 'It's decidedly unfunny, Mathilde. Now, if you think you are up to playing something other than Teutonic cadenzas on the organ, I would like to hear the affectingly simple introduction to *Angels from the realms of glory.*'

'You're being racist...' a voice called from over at the nativity crib.

'...and a bully!' accused another.

'Jawohl, mein Gauleiter!' Mathilde raised an ironic eyebrow towards the crib ladies and got a thumbs-up from them as she launched into *Angels from the realms of glory.*

'Thank you.' Stuart looked around as the carol began. A puzzled look spread across his face. 'Bloody hell!' he expostulated.

There was another hiss from the back of the church.

'Stop, Mathilde! Stop.' He glared at Alison. 'Where is Megan?

'Mother of God?' Alison said questioningly, having no idea where Megan was.

Stuart was shouting at the three wise men who seemed to be napping, lolling against each other. 'You lot,' he bellowed. 'You're in this scene. Get over here now. And where is the star of Bethlehem?'

'Still in Israel,' a voice piped up from somewhere among the crib ladies.

'Flight must have been over-booked,' another chuckled.

Alison held up her hand to the crib women, shaking her head at them. 'Sorry, it's here, Stuart.'

She took the star out of a large cardboard envelope and moved with it towards the three angels. Glitter fanned out behind her as she walked.

'Stardust! It's a miracle,' someone chortled.

'It's a mess that we'll have to clean up,' one of the two cleaning women complained.

'It'll be a miracle if this dress rehearsal ever gets going,' came the deep throaty voice from the back of the church.

Stuart went rigid, his fists clenched and his jaw set hard. Alison turned and peered down the nave. It was impossible to see anyone down there with the sun pouring in through the western windows.

'Alison.' Stuart was struggling to steady his voice. 'Do you think you can give the star to Martin and Oliver to hold, just as they have at every other rehearsal?'

Alison closed her eyes. 'Count to ten,' she told herself as the girls at the crib exploded with laughter at the glittering star.

'Sooo tacky,' someone said.

'Enough!' shouted Stuart. 'The pageant!' he pleaded, pointing at them.

The group of women closed ranks, leaning over the manger, avoiding eye contact with Stuart and shaking with laughter.

Alison thought Stuart's eyes were going to pop out of his head. Addressing nobody in particular he said in a loud, clear voice, 'And as we all know, dykes are at the cutting edge of art and design in this city. Perhaps we could have a purple and green moon with the angels in motorcycle gear.'

'Oooooh!' The crib girls erupted, this time in a burst of elated cat-calls.

'Yeah!'

'Dykes on bikes!'

'Who needs camels?'

'Can we just get on with it?' Stuart raised his hands in frustration at them and set off with a not-very-good attempt at a dignified walk to the organ.

The crib girls were left to whisper just loudly enough to irritate him. 'Silly old queen…misogynist…what's up his tush…sexist.'

He stood next to Mathilde with one hand on the organ, fingers lightly tapping a beat. There was a pause and Alison waited for Frau Kirschbaum to rip into him. Instead, with a sly grin of triumph on her face, Mathilde placed her left hand on the organ. Turning to the three angels who were standing lost in thought, she raised her eyebrows, lifted her right hand and called them to attention: 'Achtung Jungen: eins, zwei, drei!' and began to play the carol.

Jessica's rich mezzo voice filled the church with its easy grace while the boys sang a descant that Mathilde had composed for the occasion. Alison bowed her head, a spasm of such mixed emotions gripping her that she had to stand up and walk across the transept to hold herself together. Then something happened. The singing stopped, the organ trailed off. Alison turned back to see what was wrong. Jessica was standing, head bowed, her hands covering her face. Martin looked hesitant, his hands twitching as if he was going to put an arm around her, but wasn't sure it was the right thing to do. Oliver turned and stamped off to the other side of the sanctuary, muttering, 'No, no…I can't…'

Stuart stood, his facial expressions alternating between anger and confusion. 'What in the name of…?'

Then from the sun-drenched entrance of the church came another voice, a different voice from the deep male one and one that most of the congregation recognised. 'Pink! That's different. The girls look beautiful, Stuart.'

All eyes turned to the church entrance. A straight-backed, grey-haired old woman emerged out of the western sunlight framing her in a golden halo. Her voice carried down the nave. The strong Scottish accent left it in no doubt that the diminutive figure standing like the biblical Esther before her women was Marjorie Tregonning, the doyenne of the parish.

Something, a movement perhaps, feet scraping the floor, caught Marjorie's attention. She turned and peered into the gloom of the back corner. 'Tobias, is that you?'

A deep resonant voice replied. 'Good afternoon, Marjorie.'

'Ah!' Marjorie exclaimed. 'Come to spy on us for the bishop, have you?'

'Tobias!' Stuart was aghast at the revelation that the voice from the back of the church was their archdeacon, Tobias Aldridge. What is he doing here? This isn't good.

He called down the nave, putting on his best voice. 'Good afternoon, Tobias. What a pleasant surprise. Won't you join us up here?'

It struck Stuart and Alison at the same time what the cast and crew must look like to Tobias. They were such a motley mess of lesbians in overalls and young men in tight shorts or full-length caftans. They were gathered around the unfinished crib, while the figure of the infant Jesus lay between a bale of hay and an unconvincing moth-eaten donkey. Alarm spread like wildfire among them, that the pageant was about to be cancelled by the archdeacon.

'Why else would he be here?' one of the women whispered.

In the centre of the sanctuary stood the incongruous figures of two pink angels with a third standing alone over to one side.

The archdeacon stood up. His voice boomed into the heavy air of the nave. 'The bishop needs to be reassured that he isn't going to be embarrassed if he attends the nativity pageant, Stuart. I'm sure you appreciate his concern.'

Marjorie spoke up before anyone could answer. 'Tell him not to worry, Tobias. This is a Christian community first and foremost. The gay bit is their business. Private stuff.' She waved her hand with the stick at the astonished thespians, nearly dropping a huge bunch of flowers as she did so.

'We're not expecting sexual improprieties,' Tobias guffawed. 'However, from what I've seen so far, I am not convinced that you have managed to create a holy and respectful presentation of the birth of the Son of God.'

Stuart turned back to the assembled cast and crew, glaring and shaking his head, apportioning blame to them.

'Sit down, Tobias,' Marjorie ordered. 'Stuart will show just how beautiful the pageant is going to be.' She set off down the nave, her walking stick tap-tapping her progress.

Alison had the horrible thought that the tapping was like a time bomb about to go off. But there was the indomitable little woman, marching towards the sanctuary, almost invisible under her flowers: shasta daisies, sprays of fragrant artemesia, javelin-sized stems of blue and white agapanthus and clusters of pink Japanese wind anemones scattering petals like snow.

'A cornucopia of floral delights,' one of the crib girls trilled in a high falsetto, a mix of admiration and glee.

'All local in Bethlehem at the time,' another called.

'Is there anything left in her garden?' someone wondered.

'My God,' murmured Stuart, 'Birnam Wood to Dunsinane hath come. Is this an omen?'

'Stuart! Shame on you!' Oliver had spun around. 'The Scottish play! Never quote that play in a theatre.'

'It's not a theatre!' Alison spoke more vehemently than she had meant to.

Everyone turned to look at her.

'It's a church,' she added apologetically, casting a glance down the nave to where the Venerable Tobias Aldridge had disappeared back into the corner.

'A place of worship! That's the spirit,' Majorie's voice sounded exalted and entirely out of place in the tense atmosphere that had settled in the stifling heat of the afternoon.

Alison wondered if she ought to help the frail-looking old woman up the steps to the sanctuary. 'She'll never make it,' she whispered to Stuart.

But before she could move, Jessica's girlfriend, Megan, had emerged from the vestry and headed across the sanctuary to join Marjorie in the nave. She took the flowers, offered her arm to Marjorie, and escorted her safely back up the nave towards the vestry. Oliver had started to move across to do the same thing, but was now stranded next to Martin and Jessica.

'Well,' Stuart moaned, 'at least we've located the mother of the Son of God.'

When she and Megan arrived at the transept, Marjorie could see the angels at close range. The church fell silent again as she stared at the three motionless figures in their flowing pink robes and feathered wings.

Then she turned, frowning, and addressed Stuart. 'The two on the ends should wear veils. Their hair is too short. They look like boys.'

Stuart's eyes shot up towards heaven. 'That's because they are boys,' he muttered under his breath. His voice was respectful when he spoke, though Alison could hear the strain behind it. 'They are boys, Marjorie. That's the point, boys in pink,' he explained. 'Pink for girls, blue for boys! We're upending the convention here.'

Marjory's face remained blank.

'It's a gay pageant. You know,' he continued, desperate to explain the gayness to Marjorie, 'queer, same-sex, camp…boys in pink, that's the point.'

Alison put a hand on Stuart's arm and his voice trailed off.

The old lady half-turned to have a second look at the boys, but she was distracted by the star lying on the floor. 'The point? Ah yes, you're right, dear. The star is too tizzy. There is no point in having it in the pageant. The bishop won't like it.'

There was a chortle from the back of the church.

I'm not at all sure the bishop is going to like any of it, Alison thought. Why he has agreed to come to the midnight mass pageant and service at all is a mystery. He's not exactly sympathetic to sexual diversity.

'But I must give you credit for one thing, Stuart, the girls do look beautiful in pink.'

Muffled laughter rippled through the church as Marjorie proceeded up the steps and tapped across the sanctuary, smiling at the three angels as she passed by them. Her voice trailed off as she entered the vestry where taps soon could be heard filling the vases.

'It's supposed to be gay, a gay Christmas, Marjorie,' Stuart muttered feebly after her.

Jessica turned abruptly and dramatically thrust her hand towards Martin, who took it. Alison looked from them to Oliver. She wasn't at all sure that he wasn't about to burst into tears.

'Can somebody please tell me what on earth is going on?' Stuart looked at Alison, who looked at Martin, who looked away from her, first to Jessica and then to Oliver.

'Mum, Stuart, we have a problem. Can you come here?' Alison heard the tremor in his voice with some alarm.

All eyes were riveted on the three pink angels. Some of the cast began moving closer to listen. Most of the women knew what this was about, but wanted to hear Martin's version of events.

'Please,' Martin pleaded, holding up a hand, 'Just Mum and Stuart, OK?'

'And me.' It was Tobias Aldridge. He was already in the nave and advancing on the disorder and consternation as if it were Judgement Day.

Martin was mortified and Jessica dropped his hand.

Oliver spoke. His voice was firm, definite. 'No, Archdeacon! Excuse me, but this is private.' He lifted his chin, indicating the other two angels. It's between me, Martin and Jessica.'

'I'd say it's about as private as a Mardi Gras parade, young man.' Tobias had reached the front of the nave and was taking in everyone with a stern look, while at the same time allowing a wry smile to play across his face. 'I would have thought this dress rehearsal couldn't stand another upset. Now, what's the matter and let me see if I can be an impartial third party and help you sort it out so Stuart can get on with it.'

Nobody moved. 'Well, do you want a pageant tonight or not?' the archdeacon asked.

Stunned silence held them all in its thrall.

'Well then,' he turned to Martin, 'what's the problem?'

Alison swept her eyes over the three pink angels standing before her. They are so young. They're babies. Her nerves failing her, she took hold of Stuart's arm to steady herself. He glanced at her in surprise.

Martin looked at Oliver and back at Jessica. Alison knew her boy. He was marshalling his courage to say what had to be said. She smiled at Oliver, who wouldn't meet her eyes. Instead, he bent his head and stared at the floor in front of him.

'Mum, Jessica and I are trying to decide whether to hook up together. She loves me.'

'Not love,' Oliver burst out. 'It's a crush. Jessica thinks she loves you because you're nice to her. You listen to her, take her seriously. But it's all fantasy. You're gay and so is she.'

'Don't say that, Ol. I know my gay side. I love you. But Jess...'

'She has Megan,' Oliver shot back. 'Why has she come between you and me?'

'Because she's a manipulative little bitch.'

The voice came from the back of the crowded group. The cast froze, nobody turning to check who it was that had spoken. Alison couldn't tell if it was one of the crib girls or one of the boys. A sustained hissing started and grew louder, but was cut off by the booming voice of the Venerable Tobias Aldridge.

'Stop! Stop this at once. You call yourselves a Christian community, sharing a particular sexuality which is the common bond. But you are behaving like combatants, out to get the better of one another. All I've seen this afternoon is division and disarray. I came to see a dress rehearsal, but I haven't seen a single scene performed since I arrived.'

The archdeacon turned to Martin and Jessica. 'How long has this attraction been going on?'

Martin and Jessica were taken aback at the bluntness of the question. They looked away from the archdeacon.

'Since first thing this morning,' Oliver interjected. 'It's true, Marty. She started playing up to you the moment she arrived and you fell for it. It flattered your vanity.'

Tobias held up a hand. 'You're the boyfriend, I take it?'

Oliver nodded, sullen and flushed. He looked at Martin and tears welled in his eyes. 'Ex-boyfriend.'

'We want to try living together,' Martin ventured, ' the three of us. You know, a ménage à trois.'

There was a gasp from the cast and crew. A few laughed out loud and the sanctuary was filled with muted whispers, snorts of disapproval and expressions of disbelief.

Alison stared at her son, completely taken aback. 'Hook up.' 'Ménage à trois.' The words went round and round in her head without resolving into anything meaningful. Boyfriend? Girlfriend? Ex-boyfriend? What do they know of love? They're babies.

Stuart let out a long breath beside her. 'Well! And just how is that going to work?'

Alison wasn't sure whether he was speaking to her or Martin or the archdeacon. Perhaps he was just thinking aloud.

Jessica moved closer to Martin. He looked up and beckoned Oliver to come and stand on the other side of him, but the boy didn't move.

'Come on, Ol. You're part of this, babe. You know how I feel about you. Jess is prepared to give it a go and I want you there too.'

Tobias pointed a finger at Martin. 'Are you saying you're bisexual?'

Martin looked totally flustered. He'd not thought of that. The idea of loving Jessica was exciting, but it was all so new and a bit unreal.

He felt confused. Under the steady gaze of the archdeacon, he baulked for the first time since the morning at the entanglement he was getting himself into. There was Oliver on the point of tears and he wanted to go to him. But what about Jessica? And where was Megan in all this? She and Jess had been girlfriends for longer than he and Ol had been together.

Martin stepped away from Jessica, looking from her to Oliver, from Oliver to his mother standing there with her mouth open and to Stuart, who looked despairing.

Tobias turned to Oliver and motioned to him to come closer. The boy reluctantly stood next to Martin, but wouldn't look at him.

'You can't play around with love. Nor can you play around with sexuality.' Tobias let the words sink into the silence. 'You can't decide in the course of a morning that you might change your sexuality and encompass someone of the opposite sex. Life doesn't work like that.'

He addressed Martin. 'I take it you've been living together, is that right? With Oliver?'

Martin nodded.

'So now you have decided this morning that he is not enough for you. Is that right?'

Martin shook his head. 'No! I love Ollie.' He took Oliver's hand, and looked surprised when Oliver pulled it away.

Tobias pressed on. 'How do you know you love this girl?'

He turned to Jessica for the first time and addressed her. 'And how do you know you love this boy? Where has your love for Megan gone?'

The two angels blushed. The archdeacon's words were spinning round in their heads. Jessica put her hands over her mouth and looked down the nave towards the door, towards escape.

'Let me suggest a plan,' Tobias said quietly. 'Go back to living with your partners. Over the next few months, go out with each other. Go out as a foursome. Test this new love, as you call it. See if it holds. You don't have to decide anything now. You're young. You have plenty of time to see what it is you want from each other. It may be love, or it may be friendship. Time will help…and prayer.'

There was a silence.

Then the archdeacon glanced at Stuart and Alison. 'And now let's get on with the real priority for this afternoon, the dress rehearsal for the pageant,' he said.

Oliver hadn't moved. Martin and Jessica didn't know what to do.

'Ollie?' Martin spoke quietly.

'I can't do this,' Oliver said. 'I can't…won't be the odd one in a relationship. I love you, Marty, I really do, but this…?' His voice broke. He turned to the vestry, but Marjorie was blocking the doorway, where she'd heard everything.

Martin looked from Jessica to Oliver and took a step towards his boyfriend. 'Ollie, Ollie!' Martin went to him and turned him round so that they were face to face.

They began talking quietly and slowly Oliver raised his eyes to look at Martin. Jessica was left standing alone and forlorn.

'The pageant?' Stuart murmured feebly to Tobias.

'Dear Lord, is my son bisexual?' Alison was a mixture of amazement, surprise and more than a little uncertainty at the situation.

'What about the pageant? Are we going to have the pageant?' Stuart's voice was rising on an increasing note of frustration.

'Stuart, we need a toilet break.' Marjorie had come across the sanctuary and was standing in the chancel, a commanding presence brooking no opposition. With all eyes riveted on her, she said, 'We are going to have the pageant if I have anything to do with it.' She held Tobias's gaze. 'They've all worked too hard to fail and, besides, it will give the bishop a well needed wake-up call about how the parishes are constituted in the twenty-first century. Don't you agree, Tobias?'

Tobias grinned and made a small bow to her. Stuart opened his mouth to speak, but Marjorie held up her walking stick, stopping him from saying anything.

'Now,' she bade them, 'let's get this rehearsal underway.' Marjorie turned back to Jessica. 'Are you up to being an angel for us, my dear?' She didn't pause for an answer. 'Why don't you encourage your girlfriend to come up and play the mother of Christ for us. We can't have the birth of the Son of God without the mother, can we, dear?' She turned to Martin and Oliver and called, 'Girls, we're waiting for you.'

'They're boys, Marjorie,' Stuart murmured feebly. 'Boys.'

Marjorie turned to the three wise men. 'You three queens of Orient are, and if you don't need a toilet break, get into your positions. Come on, hop to it and stop flashing your underwear, young man. It's most unbecoming and we are about to begin.'

The three boys leapt into action amongst a chorus of the crib women adapting the traditional carol to sing, 'We three queens of Orient are…'

Tobias shook his head. 'Discipline, Stuart,' he growled, 'or no show.'

Stuart was nonplussed and all he could manage was 'I'm trying to direct…'

'Yes, dear,' Marjorie replied. She turned to the archdeacon. 'You've done your good deed, Tobias, and we are grateful for that. Stuart can manage from here on.' She took the archdeacon by the arm. Proceeding down the nave with the familiar tap-tapping of her walking stick, she sat them in a pew five rows back.

Alison squeezed Stuart's arm. 'I think we can all get on with it now.'

She glanced over to Martin and Oliver. Martin's arm was around Oliver's shoulder and as she watched, Oliver leaned in and put his head on Martin's neck. Looking around, she noticed Jessica and Megan were talking earnestly and Jessica was nodding at whatever it was that Megan was saying.

Stuart followed her gaze up to Martin and Oliver. Yes. A rehearsal with three angels in pink. They do look beautiful, Marjorie, he reflected, allowing his eyes to linger on Martin just that little bit longer than he should have as the two boys walked back arms around each other.

'Much ado about nothing?' he whispered to Alison with a questioning look on his face.

Alison didn't answer, watching her son with Oliver. He is so happy, she thought. That matters. He has his faith and that matters too. Dear Lord, here we are in an unusual moment in time when the behemoth of homosexuality is allowed to take centre…not stage, she stopped herself. Centre place in a church. That has to be a good thing, I guess.

'Okay! Where are we up to?' Stuart asked in an effort to exert control. He surveyed the scene confronting him and shuddered. The set was scattered in disarray across the sanctuary, the star lay on the floor amidst a slurry of glitter, shepherd crooks were piled on top of each other, the donkey had fallen over and the bale of hay was disintegrating as a result of the three wise men standing unwisely on it to get a better view of the archdeacon confronting the angels. The worst of it was the crib upturned and the baby Jesus lying half-buried under it.

'Bethlehem isn't looking too good at the moment,' he murmured. 'Action! That's what we need.' He clapped his hands three times and said in the deepest and most commanding voice he could muster, 'All right, ten minutes for the crew to get the set in order and then we are going to do a complete run-through without any mishaps.'

Nobody moved.

'Go!' he shouted. 'Don't just stand there, move.'

The front of the church erupted into a hive of activity as things were put to rights and the cast threw on what costumes they had to hand.

Alison giggled at the sight of the shepherdesses in long robes with their boots sticking out under the hems. 'Miracles happen,' she whispered to herself. 'Let's make one here tonight.'

'Positions, please, everyone,' Stuart ordered.

Mathilde Kirschbaum played the introductory carol, *On the Road to Bethlehem*, and Alison joined in, humming the lyric line.

Alison linked her arm with Stuart's and they listened to the excited chatter as the carol reverberated among the members of the rainbow congregation.

'Have we avoided a disaster,' Stuart murmured, 'the pageant versus the three angels and their gay alter egos sorting out their love lives?'

Alison patted his arm. 'Love? Isn't that what Christmas is about?'

Stuart looked at her, the strain of near failure still on his face. 'Alison, all I wanted was a good dress rehearsal and a knock-out pageant.'

'Instead, we are working towards peace on earth and goodwill to all men and women,' she grinned. 'These young people are learning what it means to be alive and to love, to sort out their relationships in all the important ways.'

He patted her arm and she felt the condescension in it. But it no longer irked her. 'Merry Christmas, Alison.'

She laughed and planted a great big kiss on his cheek. 'Merry Christmas, Stuart.'

Benediction

In the beginning was the Word, and the Word was with God, and the Word was God. The same was in the beginning with God. All things were made through him; and without him was not anything made that was made. In him was life; and the life was the light of men.

'His life is the light of men.' Brother Robert's whisper was prayer-like. 'And the life was light,' he repeated, opening his eyes to the altar, now basking in the soft, afternoon glow. The words from John 1 filled him with a profound sense of oneness with the Divine.

The smell of incense hung in the air over the altar, a pale suspension, illuminated by the sun behind the tall, amber, west-facing windows of the monastery chapel. Benediction was over, but Brother Robert remained on his knees. The glory of God was filtering into him through the words of the apostle, curling in the haze of aromatic smoke that had wafted from the shiny brass thurible.

Brother Robert inhaled, recalling the blended smells of polished wood and incense from his days in the seminary and serving in churches in his early days of Holy Orders. The memory was intoxicating, spiritual.

The priest had carried the monstrance across the sanctuary, into the Sacristy. He would disrobe, hanging the ornately embroidered chasuble in the large walnut wardrobe. He would remove the stole, kiss its cross and carefully fold it and place it in a cupboard drawer.

Brother Robert followed the clothing rituals in his mind, savouring the reassurances that habit provided. Father Donovan would wind the cincture into a neat ball and place it next to the stole. Finally, he would remove the alb, that crisp white linen symbol of purity, that representation of Christ's own precious garment. It would hang alongside the chasuble ready for use at mass the following morning.

His mind was steeped in the Benediction, the pure adoration of God. In many ways it was the service he loved most with the brilliant radials of the monstrance striking out like a glorious sunburst, the light of God. The vestments, the incense, the eye of God as he called the host in the centre of the monstrance, brought back long-ago memories of the richly decorated churches of Naples where he had worshipped with his parents as a boy before the family emigrated to Australia.

Two young altar boys, brothers as he knew them to be, had served the priest at Benediction. They had dutifully preceded him from the altar. The younger lad had been captivated by the golden gleam of the thurible with its burning centre concealed in the gleaming brass orb, exuding the heavy scent of incense. His face had been a study in solemnity that brought a tender smile to Brother Robert's face. The little boy had been swinging the thurible rather wildly from side to side, sending up clouds of aromatic smoke. He had almost stopped moving in their procession to the Sacristy.

The older lad suddenly turned and hissed at his brother to get out of the sanctuary. The hiss echoed through the chapel, unmistakable, definitely not holy. The little chap reacted immediately, almost tripping on the marble steps as he ran and disappeared through the Sacristy door. Brother Robert's smile widened. He had been an altar boy.

The other monks had filed out of the chapel along the central nave. Brother Robert remained kneeling, looking straight ahead. He did not notice the slight hesitation and inquisitive glance from the Abbot as he passed by and then continued down the aisle into the monastery's Gethsemane Garden.

The Abbot worried about Brother Robert. Recently he seemed increasingly immersed in contemplation, or perhaps he was off in other worlds of his own. The old man might be a true mystic the Abbot told himself when he was being kind. Or was he suffering from the onset of dementia? Still, he did seem to manage his duties in the garden and was always punctual at the rituals of the day.

The Abbot looked up as an Airbus 360 roared over the monastery. He put his fingers in his ears to block out the piercing scream of the engines and concentrated on the garden until it had passed. Rob certainly has a green thumb he thought. He looked across the trim, velvety green of the lawn. Vigorous spring growth was everywhere. But the winter had not been kind to Brother Robert, bringing him down with pneumonia again, two years in a row now. Why won't he agree to vaccination? 'God's will be done,' Brother Robert had replied to the suggestion. The Abbott continued on towards the house, looking forward to his cup of tea and a biscuit or two.

Brother Robert shook his head at the ruckus coming from the sacristy as the older boy railed against his younger brother and the priest tried to quieten him. So like my brother and me all those years ago, Brother Robert recollected. He could not make out the words as they echoed around the empty chapel. The words became increasingly indistinct as they bounced off the brick walls, spiralling around the tortured body of the crucified Christ hanging over the altar. He closed his eyes for a moment as the shrill children's voices became completely indecipherable. This behaviour has no place among the Stations of the Cross with their representation of unbearable suffering for humanity. If only people would really look and think about the passion of Christ. What is this altercation between the two boys compared to His agony? he reflected as the roar of an approaching jet drowned out the heated exchange.

A door slammed in the sacristy and there was silence. This was how he liked it best, just him and his Lord in God's house. Nearer my God to Thee. His eyelids fluttered as a sigh escaped his lips.

As the light dwindled towards dusk, the saints and apostles maintained their stony silence on the chapel walls. The lingering odour of incense was fading. A chill had crept into the chapel and Brother Robert shivered. He raised his eyes to the crucified Christ.

Brother Robert tried to stand up. These old joints, he thought, you have served me well in life. You think you are entitled to a rest do you?

He smiled through the pain as he eased himself back onto the seat. The effort had made him breathless. He closed his eyes, steadying his intake of air, in, out, in, out. 'Lord forgive me my sins.'

'The life is light,' he murmured. 'His life is the light of men.'

*

Adele Johnson stood at the compost bin shredding the newspapers of the last two days, dropping the thin strips into the bin. Wet, dry, green, that's the way to do compost. Well that's what the lady at the nursery had told her – or was it green, wet, dry? What does the order matter really? It's words, only words, Adele thought.

'It's only words and words are all I have…'

She sang softly to herself as she tore a sports report and picture of tough rugby players, watching their dismembered bodies and shredded sentences float into the smelly darkness of the bin.

Words, so many words she thought, so many words written about so many people and things. Finance words, rip, in you go. More use as compost than broadcast as the speculations and opinions of journalists. The crossword page, the middle pages filled with mundane reports of people and events. Rip, tear, drop – there you go. Banished to the fodder-for-plants bin.

She stepped back to catch her breath from the smell of putrefying vegetable peelings. The sun was hot and she had forgotten to put on her hat. Bugger, she thought. Nearly done though, just this last section to go. What do we have here? Oh very nice, the Obituaries, well ashes to ashes as they say. You'll do a lot better being recycled into the ground. Fertilise the dying Earth, that's really something to remember you by.

Adele opened the paper lengthways and started to tear. She suddenly stopped with an abrupt intake of breath. She turned, looking back into the garden not wanting to believe the obit she had seen. Her heart was beating quickly and she was trembling. Was it just the heat of the day…or was it what was in the obits?

She spread the paper over the recycling bin and adjusted her eyes to compensate for not having her reading glasses. Is this a trick of my eyes or has the small print taken me back into a past I have never forgotten? No, there it is as clear as it could be, even without my specs.

'Our beloved brother in Christ, Roberto Pucci, also known as Brother Robert of the Order of the Glory of Heaven, died…'

She stopped reading. Roberto, dead! That beautiful, lusty young Italian boy she had been so in love with. Those thrilling nights in the park, on beaches, making love under the stars in the heat of summer and the chill of one autumn. He was always so considerate of her feelings and pleasure. My beautiful Robbie dead! She had to sit. Under the lemon tree. Get out of the sun. Clear her head and think.

She sat, cross-legged, a teenager again. She was trying to focus her thoughts, control the emotion surging through her. Fragments from a fairy-tale past appeared amongst the hanging orbs of lemon and disappeared into the foliage around her.

The shade cooled her. In the next backyard, Josie was bawling out her little sister. She could hear their mother calling to them to stop arguing or they would have to come inside. It was all so ordinary. In the street, the young fellow six doors down started up his motorbike and quickly took off, the roar of his engine drowning out the little girls before fading off into the distance. All so ordinary, except it wasn't. Robbie was dead.

Roberto, the wog boy, the other kids used to call him. He had so little English at first and was the cause of much merriment in class. Adele used secretly to watch him, curious about a boy from that far-off land. He was all right, just a bit different. Over term one, curiosity turned to liking, turned smoothly into a fantasy of deep longing to be with him, to speak Italian, to be Italian so that she could at least listen and understand him.

The adults used to talk about the Puccis and it was clear to Adele that they were unwelcome in the neighbourhood. Greasy, her brother said. Well, actually, the worst thing was that they were Micks, Roman Catholics. But Adele didn't mind that and used to oblige her mother by going to the corner shop to buy milk just so she could see Roberto and his family going off to church on Sundays. This was despite her mother nagging that she was leaving it so late the shop would probably be shut by the time Adele got there. It was only when her younger sister blurted out that Adele went then so that she could see the Itie boy she fancied that her parents twigged to the truth.

Adele's mother was shocked and forbade Adele ever to pull such a sneaky, despicable deception on her ever again. And, she was forbidden to have anything to do with the wog boy or his family.

Then at school the very next Monday, Roberto had passed by her in the playground and stopped. 'I notta see you buy milk yesterday. I think you sick maybe.'

Adele felt her feet had left the surface of the Earth and she was floating next to the second-form classroom. She couldn't speak and just stood there, shaking her head at him. Roberto looked confused and was about to say something when she suddenly found her voice. It came out all scratchy and thin.

'No, I'm fine, thank you. I'm Adele.'

She had tried to smile but was sure it came out as pulling a face at him. He nodded. 'I know.' He was about to say something, but moved off as some of her friends came over. From that moment on, Adele knew what it meant to be in love. She was in love with Roberto Pucci, the wog boy from Italy with those beautiful eyes that she had just floated in.

After the first-term holidays, Adele and Roberto began to speak to each other more often. Her friends mocked him and tried to keep her away from him. It was the boys who took to him first when they realised his skills with a football. He was quietly accepted by them when the seniors' coach put him on the team. Even though he said in Italy they played what Australians call soccer, he was still a natural on the field and faster than any of the others. Once the boys had accepted him, the girls followed suit. Some even began to admit that he was handsome, but it was clear that Adele was the one he seemed to like most.

Then he asked her to a CYO dance. She had no idea what it was until he explained that it was the Catholic Youth Organisation, which held dances on Sunday nights and that they were good fun and would she come. She did. Her best friend covered for her, telling her mother that Adele was invited to her place for tea and card games afterwards. Roberto had escorted her back there after the dance and her friend's brother walked the two girls to Adele's house to allay her mother's suspicions.

The first time they made love, had sex really, was after a party when he was walking her home. They stopped in the park and kissed and kissed. That led to fumbling in each other's clothes and groping. Then they were lying on the grass and Roberto was on top of her. She let him enter her and she didn't care. Everything her mother had said about boys evaporated from her mind and she steeped herself in the exquisite pleasure that they were having.

It had been so special and she never regretted it.

As they left the park, Roberto was quiet, distant. She remembered thinking that she had done something wrong. Maybe he hadn't enjoyed it as she thought he had. She stopped walking and asked him.

'Yes,' he said, 'something is very wrong. What we did is a mortal sin in my religion. Very bad. We will go to Hell unless we confess.'

Adele could still recall the overwhelming urge to laugh out loud and the realisation that she mustn't.

'I don't believe that Robbie, and I am not sorry we did it.'

Whatever his religious scruples were seemed not to stem the tide of his passion for her. They moved into a sexual relationship over that summer which she could not imagine her life without. This was the boy she was going to marry. Even so, she remembered, she had always been aware of some hesitancy, something other about Robbie, but could never put her finger on what it was.

Then one day on the beach, he told her that he had been accepted into the Order of the Glory of Heaven. At first she had no idea what that was. Then when he explained it to her she was aghast. A religious order! It was incomprehensible. The words echoed around in her head but she could not make sense of them. How could he shut himself off from the world, from people, from her? And what about sex? He loved sex.

Try as he might, Roberto could not explain the drive in him to devote his life to God. Adele had never understood it. She had been shattered for years by his decision and now, here it was back again, the sense of abandonment, except he was dead. He had stayed with his God and now he was with his God.

Adele stood up and went back to the compost bin. She read the obituary notice again and let the tears fall onto the paper. She wiped her eyes on her sleeve and resumed shredding.

'It's only words and words are all I have…'

Adele sank to her knees and wept.

The Immutable Shadows of Men

Long before he died, Harry had stopped wearing his watch. Funny I should think of that now. He'd always worn it, even when he was at work, playing squash or swimming. Even in bed. Sometimes when we were making love – was it love or just sex? – it would scratch me and I'd make him take it off before I'd let him go on. After we'd stopped having sex, Harry stopped wearing the watch.

Was there a connection? Was he timing our lovemaking?

The strange thing about his watch is that Harry was never on time.

I can't really see him now that he's dead, but in my mind's eye I can imagine what he'd be doing. Pissing on the camellias, that's what. I can see his shadow on the lawn, his right arm, a grey fuzzy blur, crooked, holding himself, holding that weapon of mass destruction that he used on me – and on the camellias. I can just see his left hand up to the wrist, steadying himself against the wall. And the watch is not there. What happened to the watch?

So esoteric, that's what Harry was. He once read in the newspaper about a railway station in Osaka that had a magnificent hedge of azaleas outside it. The report indicated that the local taxi drivers used the hedge as a latrine to relieve themselves, day and night. The nitrogen and uric acid apparently nourished the plants. Harry was one of the great nourishers of nature.

Oh yes, there was that other pissing story, in a newspaper, where else. An English county soccer team used to go back to one member's house after training, for drinks and a barbecue. They used to piss on the lemon tree at the back of the garden and that tree produced bumper crops of lemons, year after year. Harry was enthralled and he took to doing the like. What if that report wasn't true?

I don't know whether Harry was more obsessed with newspapers or urine. He was certainly fixated on both. Why would Harry have read those items? Why would any journalist have reported them? Why did he feel the need to tell me when I was the one having to tidy up the disarray of newspapers and magazines strewn around the house?

Is this peculiarity, this fascination with urine, unique to the Japanese and English? I would rather it had stayed far away in those unhappy isles. Then we might have avoided the embarrassment of his sharing these miracles of horticultural ephemera with any poor unsuspecting visitor who made the mistake of commenting on the garden.

It was difficult to like Harry at times. Most of the time, in fact. But I'm sure I loved him. After all, one can't measure something like that in dirty cups and plates. There's got to be more to love than overcoming inconvenience.

Teaching myself to stop crying helped. Though I don't think it improved our love. No, it was more a case of strengthening my tolerance of his antics.

His capacity to create mess, any kind of mess, was phenomenal. Used mugs, plates just plonked on the bench when he'd finished with them. The dishwasher is next to the sink, but could he find his way to putting the plates and things in there? No. And if it wasn't crockery then it would be opened envelopes, lids off jars, paper bags and wires. Where did the wires come from? What did he want with them? Usually I threw them into the hard-waste recycling bin after a few days. Then, Harry would invariably come into the kitchen and say, 'I put some wires here. What happened to them?'

I realised early on in our marriage that it was better to feign ignorance than tell him I got rid of them. When in my youthful naivety I used to tell the truth, he would carry on for hours about my wastefulness.

Another thing was his ability to colonise any available space. Any empty surface was soon covered with his magazines, books he was reading, piles of bills waiting to be paid. These could accumulate on coffee tables, couches, the dining room table, the bed and one time even on the stove top. I had a powerful urge to turn on the gas jet and set fire to the lot. But my fear of burning the house down prevailed.

I can see the camellias now out of the window. They seem to be doing very nicely without his ministrations. And the surfaces inside! They are clear so I can put the things I want on them without the concern of interfering with his mess.

Ah, there's the postie. I'll just go and check the mailbox.

Brrr! It's chilly outside.

The house feels eerie. Is it the winter chill sending shivers down my spine? Maybe it's these morose thoughts about him that are affecting me. Every time I look at his lounge chair, the depression his body made in it jerks back memories of him. They're not all good.

Who'd have thought the memory of Harry would have that much power over me? It's just that it is getting on to that time of year when a body wants to snuggle up with another with the heating on and a hot meal in your tummy. Not that Harry and I really had that level of intimacy. He had it for the kids, rarely for me. Only when I asked for a cuddle and that wasn't very often. I'd ask for a cuddle now if he was here. I wonder if he'd oblige?

Do I miss Harry? Is it possible I miss his mess, his forays into hoarding? I certainly learnt to live with all that.

The sitting room looks a bit bare, I suppose. The kitchen benches – well, they look…denuded.

No! These thoughts are a symptom of bereavement. This is how a house should look, clean, tidy and presentable. Presentable? To whom? Certainly to the kids. No, they wouldn't care, actually. To be honest, they are little tarred with the Harry mess gene.

They loved him, the kids. And he certainly loved them. Even from an early age he would spend hours playing with them, building towers with coloured blocks which were left lying on the floor when the tower was abandoned. Or tipping the pieces of a puzzle on the dining table and sitting with them, putting the pieces together. I never knew where

I was going to serve the meal. But Harry was in seventh heaven with the table dominated by the puzzle and woe betide if I accidentally vacuumed up a piece or kicked a block under the dresser where it was well nigh impossible to retrieve.

You certainly knew family lived here when Harry was around with the kids. The chaos, the noise! He had them laughing so hard I was always afraid they might laugh themselves into an asthma attack. They never did though.

I kept the house clean and I kept the children clean. I dusted and vacuumed every day and I bathed the children and washed their clothes. They always looked…presentable.

Presentable! That word is a life sentence: feed the man, wash and iron his clothes; feed and clothe the kids, get them off to school on time, homework done and into bed, Saturday soccer and ballet; keep the house spick and span.

And Harry would be in his shed or the garden. At times like that he was a shadowy presence. Then he would burst back into the house after I had spent an hour tidying it and it all began again.

I sometimes wondered if Harry loved me. He expended so much emotional energy on the kids, there hardly seemed enough love left for me. I loved him. I think I did. Something like that is hard to tell, really, especially as I spent so much time resenting the way his lifestyle made things so difficult.

'He's a big personality. You're lucky to have a man like that. I'll swap if you want.' That's what my sister said to me one day when I plucked up the courage to complain about Harry's selfishness. That shocked me. Family can disappoint when you most need it.

Does this room disappoint? It does look a bit bare. Flowers! That's what it needs, a nice vase of flowers. And, why not a magazine on the coffee table? There, that looks better. Perhaps two magazines or rather, one of the classy art books that Harry liked so much. Yes, I must admit that does look good. They give the room a bit of personality. I don't want clutter, but a magazine and an art book beside a vase of flowers when I get them will give it the lived-in look.

While I'm on this roll, it was probably silly of me to put the fruit bowl in the fridge. Why don't I get it out and put it on the bench where Harry used to put it? Yes, that looks nice, more homely and there's plenty of space for when I bring a basket or two of shopping home. I can still put them here and unpack them.

And why not the newspaper here, where I can read it while having a cuppa? But neatly folded so that it doesn't take up all the bench space.

I'll put the kettle on now. Noisy thing, but it doesn't take long to boil. Harry seemed to be boiling it all the time when he was around. He liked his tea. He wasn't the only one. I do, too.

My gosh, look at that headline. Wow! Harry would have been interested in this. Let's spread the paper out so I can read the report while the tea's brewing.

www.ingramcontent.com/pod-product-compliance
Lightning Source LLC
Chambersburg PA
CBHW051228210726
48290CB00003B/852